The Correspondent

The Correspondent

A Novel

Virginia Evans

CROWN
NEW YORK

CROWN
An imprint of the Crown Publishing Group
A division of Penguin Random House LLC
crownpublishing.com

Library of Congress Cataloging-in-Publication Data
Names: Evans, Virginia, 1986- author. Title: The correspondent : a novel / Virginia Evans.
Identifiers: LCCN 2023053777 | ISBN 9780593798430 (hardcover ; acid-free paper) | ISBN 9780593798454 (trade paperback ; acid-free paper) | ISBN 9780593798447 (ebook) Subjects: LCGFT: Epistolary fiction. | Novels. Classification: LCC PS3605.V3774 C67 2025 | DDC 813/.6—dc23/eng/20231120
LC record available at https://lccn.loc.gov/2023053777

Hardcover ISBN 978-0-593-79843-0
International edition ISBN: 979-8-217-08643-6
Ebook ISBN 978-0-593-79844-7

Editor: Amy Einhorn
Editorial assistant: Lori Kusatzky
Production editor: Natalie Blachere
Text designer: Andrea Lau
Production managers: Philip Leung and Heather Williamson
Copy editor: L. J. Young
Proofreader: Vicki Fischer
Publicist: Lindsay Cook
Marketer: Kimberly Lew

Manufactured in the United States of America

7th Printing

Art appearing on pages ii–iii: Shutterstock.com/Vitalino11

First Edition

To Mark, with love

What I have made for myself is personal,
but is not exactly peace. . . .
Most of us live less theatrically, but remain the survivors of
a peculiar and inward time.

Joan Didion, "On the Morning After the Sixties,"
The White Album

The Correspondent

A PREFACE

At last, on Monday around ten or half past, Sybil Van Antwerp carries the mug of Irish breakfast tea with milk to her desk. The bed is made, the dishes clean and drying on a towel beside the sink, the plants watered, the shelves dusted. She scoots the chair with precision, then gazes for a few moments out the window over her garden and toward the river off and below, at the few white triangle sails there in the distance, the reflection of the sky on the wide water, the square mansions on the Annapolis side. With satisfaction, she straightens the stack of letter-writing paper and the short, always-turning-over pile of books she will read next. She arranges the pens in the mug. She counts her stamps. She consults the stack of what letters she has received and not yet answered; a list she keeps of letters she means to write; a stack of upside-down pages in the drawer, a letter she has been writing going on years now, still unsent. Sybil is a mother and grandmother, divorced, retired from a distinguished career in law, these things are all there around her, but it is this correspondence—

On Wednesday it's the same.

And on Friday.

And on Saturday.

On Monday around ten or half past Sybil Van Antwerp sits down at her desk again. It is the correspondence that is her manner of living.

Felix Stone
7 Rue de la Papillon
84220 Gordes
FRANCE

June 2, 2012

Felix, my dear brother,

Thank you for the birthday card, the fountain pen, and the book, which I started the day it arrived (Thursday) and finished today. It was exactly as you described. Unlikely and electric, inventive, and right up my alley. Seventy-three feels the same as seventy-two for what it's worth, arthritis, constipation, and trouble sleeping, and I've decided to stop dyeing my hair. I don't care much for my birthday, as you know, though it's always nice of you to acknowledge it. Trudy and Millie of course came for appetizers and cards. The children both contacted me—Bruce had a strawberry tart delivered from a bakery (he'll be up next weekend to clean out my gutters anyway), and it was awful, so I threw it out. Probably cost him a fortune. Fiona called from London. She said she won't come home again until Christmas because work is keeping her jumping and now she is designing something in Sydney, for heaven's sake, so she'll spend a month in Australia. She assured me Walt doesn't mind how often she is gone, but I'll tell you, I don't know how their marriage will make it. She'll certainly never be able to have children at this point. (They're not even trying. At least she hasn't told me if they are. When I bring it up she chastises me.) Theodore Lübeck down the street brought me cut roses from his bushes, as he does every year, which is good of him, even if he is a renegade from the lawless fringe of the American West.

How is France? How is Stewart? What are you writing? Thank you for the invitation to visit, you're always good to refresh it. Yes, I loved <u>The Château</u>, but that was a novel, and as much as I would love to see your new house, no, I'll not come. Just as a summer afternoon is gorgeous from inside air-conditioning, and you step into the day, hot, muggy, miserable, a postcard of France with all the lavender and sunflowers, I imagine, is far more alluring than the place itself. It's such a hassle to fly these days with the security and all the regulations about the size of bag and transferring the creams and contact lens solution into the small bottles. Honestly, it doesn't appeal to me in the least, and I made it clear when you moved continents I wouldn't be coming.

I was going through boxes and found this photograph (encl.) from the day they brought you home from the Sisters. Your little trousers and absolutely bald head. You've come full circle. Mother looks gorgeous here and I've never seen another photo of her in this green skirt suit, but I remember it clearly. I remember that day as clearly as if it were yesterday. I remember there had been a bad storm, no rain, but a strange wind and warm temperatures and there was a tree down in the yard and branches and sticks, and I remember the neighbor, Mrs. Curry, had made a dinner of pot roast and a chocolate pie and I'd been waiting all afternoon for the car to pull up and bring you. Mitsy hadn't been able to get there for the morning chores because the storm had downed the lines on the Canton bridge, so I had dusted, made the beds, drawn the drapes. Can you think of who it would have been taking the photo? Mother's sister Heloise was there looking after me, but I can't imagine Heloise taking photographs. I suppose this is our first family portrait. I'm giving it to you, as I have my own photo of the day they brought me in.

My regards to Stewart, of course,
from your loving sister,
Sybil

Postscript: Felix, I got into a little scrape last night. It was nothing, really, I'm fine, but the Cadillac is in the shop. More of an inconvenience than anything else, honestly.

June 2, 2012

Dear Mr. Lübeck,

Thank you for the exquisite white roses you left on my porch on my birthday, May 29. Furthermore, I received your voice message this morning. I was delivered home by taxi last night due to a minor car accident, but everything is being taken care of.

Regards,

Sybil Van Antwerp

Ms. Ann Patchett
c/o Parnassus Books
3900 Hillsboro Pike
#14
Nashville, TN 37215

June 2, 2012

Dear Ann,

I am writing to congratulate you on your most recent novel, <u>State of Wonder</u>, which was given to me for my birthday by my brother. I finished reading it this morning. Today is Saturday and I only started the book Thursday, which says something in itself, though you wouldn't know that as we are strangers, though not utter strangers, as we have exchanged letters on one previous occasion, and that was when I read your first big smash <u>Bel Canto</u> in the very early part of the millennium and you sent a reply, remarking on my penmanship and encouraging me to address you by your first name. You might, though perhaps not, depending on the volume of letters you receive and read on a regular basis, recall from that letter that I enjoyed <u>Bel Canto</u> very much, but this new book is even better. (I should add, for clarity's sake, that I did write to you when I finished reading the book before this one, <u>Run</u>, but I never heard back, but that's just fine, so don't give it a second thought.)

It typically takes me four days to read a novel of standard length, but I was flying through the pages of <u>State of Wonder</u>, that exotic Amazonian backdrop and those smart, tremendously complex women Drs. Singh and Swenson. How did you come to be so knowledgeable about these things—the details about the Amazon, all the science—? Did you travel there? I found myself wondering about the balance of fact and fiction with the matter of the tree bark. The scene when the behemoth snake comes up from the water onto the boat and wraps its muscular snake body around the child Easter with the Americans looking on in horror, the silence of that scene was positively cinematic. I didn't take a breath for what was it then, five pages or more. And of course, the matter of Dr. Swenson, at her age (my age! Dr. Swenson is seventy-three, and so am I) being pregnant. I can't imagine. When they retrieve the baby there near the end, well that sent a chill right down my spine, but it was wonderful to read such a complex woman of her vintage, bold with her intelligence and dignity as well as her errors, and the layers upon layers of her. I am not a scientist; my own career was in law, but I saw some reflection of myself in her. The agonizing ethical questions for which the reader puts her on trial. That amazement one feels at this stage of life—a sort of astonishment that is also confusion, which leads to a sort of worry, or a sort of fear, I guess. How did we get here? How can it be? My sister-in-law Rosalie and I exchange books, and I am positive she'll love this one, so that's perfect.

Please keep in mind if you ever visit Annapolis, I'd be glad to host you. I have a small house, tucked away in a charming old neighborhood where the homes are well spaced and with massive old trees, you know. It faces the water on a point, and the upstairs is a nice big guest room with its own lavatory and a dormer window that looks toward the Severn River so you can see the boats and the large homes across the way and my garden, which I tend meticulously, there below the window. I live alone, and furthermore, I only ever go upstairs to clean after I've had company, so it's completely private and I think you would be very comfortable there. I am not a writer, but if I was I think it would be a nice place to write a book, so again, you are very welcome if you ever visit. Just a stone's throw from DC.

Until the next book, or your visit,
and with warm regards I write,

Sybil Van Antwerp

I wrecked the car. I was coming from a presentation at the library, and it was night, and I ran into a low concrete wall. The vehicle is most likely irreparable, according to the mechanic. I am fine in the body, but it's given me an awful shake. An awful shake. Of course the accident itself—the sound, the result of the Cadillac reduced to scrap,—but also because what happened is that— what happened. I'm not sure I. Well

What I think happened is that as I was driving out of the library parking lot, away from the lights and into the darkness, you know, well—I suppose I can't say exactly what happened. I was driving just like usual, slow and steady, but something occurred. I can't remember it exactly, but what I think is that quite suddenly <u>I couldn't see</u>. I couldn't see! But how? That stretch of time, was it a moment or was it minutes? It was as if my life was a movie and went black, wasn't it, but I'm not certain, and that's what's troubling me. I'm not certain it was my vision, that black chasm. It wasn't as if I'd closed my eyes; it's as if the space of time has been deleted from my memory, up until I crashed. And this has happened to me before, this feeling of deletion. That's what makes me afraid. How does a thing like that happen? I suppose it must be underway, Colt—the loss of vision. I suppose that must be what this was. I have known conceptually I would go blind, but as an eventuality. Now it seems the blinding is underway, and this is how it will go, but I didn't anticipate it being like this. This confusion.

The car went by tow, I was delivered home by a cab, and I sat awake all night afraid of the darkness. Afraid to turn off the lights.

I have nightmares. I may have mentioned this. In the nightmares I can still see, but I know I am blind somehow. So I am looking out the window at the sailboats, but maybe they are fuzzy, or maybe I know it's daytime, but it looks like night. Or I'm in the garden and I don't recognize the flowers—What is this?, I think. Or I'm looking at the text in a novel but I cannot make any sense of the letters or the words. But the worst dream, this is the one I have over and over, is I'm sitting down at the desk to write and there is the stack of letter writing paper, there are my pens, there are the envelopes, and I'm pawing at them like a cat, but I cannot pick them up. Or I pick up the pen and it lists like a noodle in my hands. I press the thing to the page and it softens or disintegrates. Or there is one version where I get as far as the ink on the page, but I can't make sense—I can't write a thing, it's all scribbling. It's the way my fear imagines blindness. You'd think the dreams would just be a black void, which is what I suppose it will actually be, though if I were dreaming of a black void I suppose . . . I wouldn't be dreaming at all. I would be simply asleep, but I don't think I sleep, at this point in my life, without dreams, the mind being far too saturated for that. Far too many haunts for that.

My ophthalmologist Dr. Jameson said that with my condition, once it gets going, it could be a year or it could be ten years until it's complete, and as things progress it can sort of come in and out. I will have to make an appointment. I'll do that today. I haven't told anyone other than Rosalie and the child Harry I've mentioned in the past, the child with whom I exchange monthly letters, son of my former colleague Judge James Landy. Oh, I've also told Joan Didion the author. I haven't told Bruce or Fiona.

TO: grandmaalicelivingston@yahoo.com
FROM: sybilvanantwerp@aol.com
DATE: Jun 2, 2012 1:00 PM
SUBJECT: Regarding Garden Club meeting June 4

Dear Alice,

Please accept my regrets for the garden club meeting this Monday, June 4. I am sorry to miss the presentation about soil pH and its effect on growing hydrangeas, however, I have an appointment that cannot be moved.

I will look forward to July.

Additionally, if there is a vote taken at the meeting Monday (June 4) regarding moving from the Sunday school room to the basement of the church in order to accommodate a larger number of attendees, I vote a very enthusiastic "NAY." The club has already grown so large as to become unwieldy. One can hardly hear during the social quarter of an hour. Furthermore, the basement is musty, probably riddled with mold, and the church board has not yet prioritized the necessary renovations that would make the space usable.

Warm regards,
Sybil Van Antwerp

TO: sybilvanantwerp@aol.com
FROM: Fiona.VanAntwerpBeau@cgemarchitects.com
DATE: Jun 25, 2012 03:31 AM
SUBJECT: Hi from Sydney

Mom, I caught up with Bruce on the phone last night and he told me you totaled the Cadillac. Why didn't you tell me when we were texting? He said you ran into a barrier of some kind (??) but you're OK (??) Were you not able to see it, or were you confused in some way? Seems . . . unlike you. Bruce said you're fine and you don't need to be seen by a doctor, but Walt and I were thinking maybe you should get checked over. I'm not trying to boss you around, but it's worrying.

I know Bruce has mentioned you moving to be closer to him. Have you given that any thought? You'd be able to see Bruce and Marie and the kids more easily, and he's said he'd love for you to be there. I've done some research, and there is actually a really nice retirement village a mile or two from his house called Happy Hills (you can click the link). They have openings in both the independent cottages (yard) and the condos (no yard), and the pay structure is kind of complicated, but your house will sell high despite the lack of updating because those waterfront lots are in such high demand. I would be happy to make some calls to get more information for you if that would be helpful. Maybe just think about it.

I should be back in London by the end of July. Let's talk on the phone then. My schedule here is packed and the time change makes it harder. Talk soon,

Fiona

Ms. Van Antwerp
17 Farney Rd.
Arnold, MD
21012

July 1, 2012

Dear Ms. Van Antwerp,

Thank you for including the <u>Expert Puzzles</u> book with your last letter. I like it very much, and I was able to complete all but three of the ciphers. How are you? Did you get a new car to replace the one you crashed? I am doing mostly fine. Here is what happened in June:

1. My parents got me a puppy (FINALLY) after I was begging for nine years. She is a golden retreiver and her name is Thor after my favorite Greek god, the god of war.

2. We are going to take a safari trip in Botswana over Thanksgiving break because my sister Susannah is working for the Peace Core there.

3. My science fair project won second prize. Thank you for helping me with the paper. The judges said my research was flawless, but there was a girl younger (sixth grade! What!) than me who built an entire robotic whale that could swim in water. My mom said it was a sure thing her parents helped her because her dad is an engineer, and my parents did not help me, so I should be proud and feel like a first place winner, which is really stupid because I didn't win, but also I agree with her somewhat.

4. My psychiatrist Dr. Laura had to move to Alaska because her husband works for an oil company, which is repugnant and I told her so, and he got relocated. I

have a new psychiatrist named Dr. Oliver and I hate him. He has bad breath and there are flakes on the top of his head and one huge disgusting scab, so every time he looks at his notepad to write down things I have to look at it and it makes me want to throw up. I am trying very hard not to say anything to him about it, and Mom says every time I go, if I keep it inside, she'll take me to pick out a candy bar at 7-11 as a reward. I made it through the first appointment, no problem, and got a Twix. Dr. Laura made me feel less weird than I really am, but Dr. Oliver makes me feel more weird than I really am (I think).

I can't wait to recieve your letter on July 15. I would also like you to check your used bookstore for any more of the older science fiction like what you sent me for Christmas, namely, H. G. Wells.

Warm regards,

Harry Landy

Postscript: I will keep your stones. I like using this code word for secrets, too. I am a very good stone keeper. I have not told anyone, not my dad or anyone, that you are going blind. Why is it a secret?

Postscript 2: Do you think President Obama will win a second term in office?

Sybil Van Antwerp
17 Farney Rd.
Arnold, MD 21012
USA

July 18, 2012

Syb,

France is splendid! You're missing out. Stewart lies around in his swimsuit all day reading magazines and he cooks at night. It's bliss. I'm working on a serial for the Times a bit and riding my bike every day (only at a moseying pace; don't get to thinking I exert myself), and I walk to the shops every afternoon for bread and cheese. I'm slim again, despite the food and wine.

You'll wear the gray well (hopefully it'll go silver), but don't cut it short at the same time; too much shock at once. My suggestion is to keep it shoulder length.

You better not say those kinds of things about her marriage to your daughter with things already strained—your own marriage was a filthy sewer even though you were home from work every night by six. It's a different time and plenty of women are having children into their forties.

The photo is great. Thank you. I've framed it and set it in the parlor and all my friends love it. They can't believe, with my accent, I'm Irish. When I take time to think about it, you know it really is something, two orphans like us, ending up Stones, living in a house with maid service. Real life rags to riches. You look wise for nine, but grave, as you always did. That neat little bob and your loafers and jumper like a doll, and then that expression on your face! It kills me. Your watchful little look, the way your little mouth is set. I feel I remember you so clearly as a child, but it's not possible. I only know you through photographs.

                                        Heading up to Paris
                                        next week for a few shows,
                                        Xxxx,

                                        Felix

Forgot—all OK with the car?

Rosalie Van Antwerp
33 Orange Lane
Goshen, CT 06756

August 10, 2012

Dear Rosalie,

I haven't heard from you. Waiting for your response to my last, but cannot wait forever. I own your life is busier than my quiet one, so I'm humbling myself and writing again. Did Paul's new wheelchair arrive? And how is Lars holding up?

Listen to the latest from my own thankless offspring. You remember I mentioned I was in a little car accident. Well, it's all sorted and I was due for an upgraded vehicle, so now I'm driving a modern Volkswagen Beetle (looks like something out of the future, a lovely red) but nearly a month after the fact I receive an e-mail from my daughter. She happens to be not in London but in Sydney, Australia, so the e-mail arrives in my inbox at four in the morning, and the meat of it is that FROM HALFWAY ACROSS THE EARTH she has heard from her brother that I was in a wreck and she has plenty of advice to give me, not the least of which is that I ought to sell my house (which she deems old, out of date) and move into a nursing home. Makes a suggestion about my financial security (and that is PRECISELY why I've never told the children what I'm worth, dollars and cents). Apparently it's something they've been discussing behind my back. As a matter of fact, Guy and I heard a case in oh, I don't know, the late eighties, and it was a woman just a touch older than myself SUING her CHILDREN because they'd duped her into selling her house and installed her into a place that was more like a prison or an insane asylum than a home for old people. Rats in the toilets, that sort of thing. Real hell for this woman. I can still picture her. Elizabeth Franklin was her name, teensy little thing sitting up on the stand and holding up her handbag, which had been chewed by rats at night. Vile. Never in twenty lifetimes would I have thought it would be me, my own children. Now I'm sure you're wondering how I replied: I did not. She is back from Sydney, rang me last week—I saw her calling and let the thing go straight to the machine. That child is brazen as brass, I'll give her that. Nerve enough to sink the Titanic. Can you imagine? She has not one single thing to do with my life, might as well live on another planet, sees me once a year if I'm lucky, and thinks it's time for me to move into a brand new nursing home in Falls Church! Well. I will do no such thing.

Pivoting. I wrote to Ann Patchett when I finished reading State of Wonder, and yesterday morning there was a reply in my mailbox! An adorable little postcard with a dog. I always love to get a note back. I am reading Cutting for Stone by Abraham Verghese (I had to look how to spell that one). It's very long. What are you reading?

Love,

Sybil

The Honorable Judge James Landy
98 Dumbarton St. NW
Washington, DC 20007

September 3, 2012 (Labor Day)

Dear James,

First things first. How is Harry doing? In his last letter I did think he seemed awfully melancholy. It's good you finally got the child a dog, but I think you also need to get him a different therapist than this Dr. Oliver. The man sounds dreadful. Are you certain he's not a pedophile? And as a matter of fact, as long as we're on the matter, you know I really don't even think Harry needs a psychotherapist. Leave it to your generation to take someone who is absolutely brilliant and turn it into a problem.

Now I'm sure you heard, but in case you hadn't, and in case you've gone down the toilet like the rest and are failing to maintain a proper newspaper subscription (IN PRINT, adequately edited, without the muck of advertisements blinking away) and only saw it on the internet, I've included the obituary. (Guy died over the weekend.) The article is a bit bland, watered down, evidently striving for the neutral language that won't stir up one political spat or another, but the photo is nice with the courthouse in the background. I think it's the same photo the papers ran when he retired. He looks very distinguished. Imagine, I thought him decrepit back then, HA, and now I'm almost the age he was.

I'd gone to see him oh, I don't know, maybe a few months ago now. You know, I don't typically travel. I go out to a few places, but I don't journey. Bruce gave me a GPS system for my car last year and it even speaks to you. Do you have one of these? It's very clever. You plug in an address and adhere the device to the windshield by suction cup, and the map moves along with you and the English voice says 'turn left here, turn right in one hundred feet,' so it would be easy for me to use it, but I don't. I'm not sure why I don't, but anyway the point is that I'd gone to visit him. (Guy, I'm talking about. He has been exclusively at his house on the bay there the last few years.) Had to drive across the Bay Bridge. I'll say I hate to drive across the Bay Bridge. I always have. Four miles, so high up it makes you sick, I was gripping the wheel. Oh, my sons used to find it so funny, if we'd drive over for the day, how I couldn't speak on that bridge. Anyway, he sat with me for about a half hour before he was tired out, and honestly most of his mind was already gone. It's a hell of a thing, to lose one's mental faculties. Guy never forgot a case, not ever, but then this series of strokes and a heart attack last year. You think of all the years, all the cases between us, this memory we shared. Honestly, I hated to go, it was very disturbing. When I first got to the house he was trying to hit on me like I was some call girl, although eventually the mists did seem to clear. He said something about the courthouse, so I knew he'd found his way back there in his mind. I was really going for Liz. I haven't spoken to her since, but it was obvious he wouldn't last much longer. Dear God, if I hope I don't live to be ninety-three. A nightmare.

The Sun did a big spread about him yesterday and you'll never believe it, but Alex Toole featured ME in her What Ever Happened To column (you cannot believe this): 'What Ever Happened to Sybil Van Antwerp?' You know I saw it there in print and I gasped. Honestly, the absurdity of it. Can you imagine? (I couldn't have. Not in a million years. Absolutely absurd.) Journalist said she tried to contact me; she most certainly did not, but even if she had I would not have dignified it with a response. The thing is foolishness, but I bought a few extra copies of the paper to be able to send the obituary, et al., to the children, Felix, etc., so it's enclosed here with the obit because I knew YOU would get a kick out of it.

How's Marly? How are the girls? Harry said you'll be traveling to Africa. You'll need to make sure you have your proper vaccinations. How's Washington? (Honestly, from my angle Washington is looking like a carnival on fire, but what else is new? I will say, it surprises me how much I like President Obama. He's a wonderful speaker, I could listen to him read the phone book.) I'm fine. It's been a nice summer. My dahlias are splendid, I am very pleased. And look, this is what I've been reduced to, an old woman writing with gardening reports while you crack on at the center of the world trying to keep the ship right.

It'll be fine to see you, presuming you will be at the funeral. The paper says they are postponing the ceremony, which is, frankly, gauche. To leave the dead in limbo like that, but nobody is consulting my opinion.

Warm regards,

Sybil

Enclosure

What Ever Happened to Sybil Van Antwerp?
Baltimore Sun Opinion/Editorial
by Alex Toole, Columnist

The honorable Judge Guy D. Donnelly of Frederick, Maryland, and St. Michaels, Maryland, has died. Judge Donnelly will be well known to many after his twenty-eight-year service to the Circuit Court of Maryland in Frederick County (1971–1999), a sober, thoughtful man of very few words who ruled with a crystal-clear justice, respected by both sides of the line, a renowned feminist. In other words, a unicorn in modern times. He died in his home with two women at his side: his wife, Elizabeth, and his daughter, Nancy Louise (married name Young), but what ever became of the other woman in his life?

In all of my research into Donnelly and his history as a judge, there she is again and again, her name spoken in every interview; her initials on documents; her face there in sketches of the courtroom; her small frame, glasses, neat pumps, even, in a photo of the judge leaving the courtroom after the explosive case of the *State of Maryland v. James Ross*, a murder case that ascended to the national stage in 1982. Sybil Van Antwerp was well known to have served as Judge Donnelly's chief clerk for almost thirty years. They retired on the same day in 1999, and there is very little information about who she was, outside of her position in relationship to the judge. She seems, as a matter of fact, to have disappeared into thin air.

Details known include: Van Antwerp graduated from law school at the University of Virginia (UVA), top of her class, in 1967, the year after the conclusion of the grueling, public *Thackery Materials v. Harold Boyne* case in which Guy Donnelly (then attorney in private practice) represented the victims. For reference, this was a case pertaining to asbestos used in naval ships as a fire retardant and the resulting asbestosis in hundreds of navy men decades after the conclusion of their service. Donnelly, now highly sought-after, with more work than he could manage, was looking for a partner, and a close friend of his, a former attorney and faculty at UVA Law, contacted Donnelly to suggest he bring on Sybil Van Antwerp with her acuity, disposition, and dogged work ethic.

Donnelly and Van Antwerp Legal was formed, and according to several people with whom I spoke, the pair shared a spark right off the bat. Sybil Van Antwerp, twenty years his junior, quickly became his collaborator. They worked hand in hand on every case. "It was like they shared a brain," Elizabeth Donnelly said. "She was his sounding board, his voice of reason. She was his equal. His work wife, they used to call her. I didn't mind; he needed her."

In 1971 Guy Donnelly was appointed to the Circuit Court of Maryland in Frederick. Faced with the prospect of maintaining the firm they had built, finding a new partner or finding another firm in the midst of raising her three young children, Sybil Van Antwerp chose the fourth option. She went with him. She left the prestige of their firm and all that money, and fell in behind Donnelly as a lowly clerk. In a *Washington Post* article from the time, the journalist mentioned contacting Van Antwerp for comment and getting her refusal. They closed the firm in short order and she followed Donnelly to the courts as his chief clerk.

"Everyone was shocked," Watts Doyle, principal attorney at the firm Ridley, Doyle, Mack & Loughlin and a friend of Donnelly's and Van Antwerp's said when I reached him by phone in Key Largo, where he is spending his retirement. "It just wasn't done. As a clerk you didn't make any money, and she was very successful by then. It really surprised us. Everyone, I mean. But in some ways, it didn't. You really couldn't imagine them ever splitting up. Butch and Sundance." And later, "An opinion from them—it'd be as clean and neat as a pin. If you sat with them for even a short time, you could see they were intellectual counterparts. They were a closed circuit. A duo. He respected her more than he respected anyone else. People used to say if she'd have been a man, she'd have been the judge. She was brilliant."

As we reflect upon the tremendous life and work of Judge Guy D. Donnelly, I cannot help but wonder after his lionized clerk. What was the full extent of their partnership, and furthermore, as charming as this perfected collaboration sounds, as idyllic, is a judgeship a position meant to be shared? Or, rather, is not this the nature of the concept of judicial install-ment, the entrusting of sentencing to an elected or appointed *individual*?

Van Antwerp disappears from the public record after her retirement, though it is purported she lives in or near Annapolis, Maryland. I sought a way to reach her, extending every resource, and found no phone number or email address.

Alex Toole
c/o <u>The Baltimore Sun</u>
300 East Cromwell Street
Baltimore, MD 21230

September 7, 2012

To: Alex Toole
From: Sybil Stone Van Antwerp, subject of your most recent
    column, OFF THE RECORD

Dear Ms. Toole,

I'd like to start by saying this letter is a matter of personal contact,
off the record—don't even think about putting any of this in your
column, bemoaning the already tired subject of who I am. I assure you, there is no audience for this.

    Secondly, it seems unlikely that you "extended every re-
source" in order to contact me, because I'm here at my house
where I have lived for many years and my address is a matter of
public record. I do not list a phone number, and there is probably
no record of my e-mail address, which indicates that is where
you stopped.

    Thirdly, and now getting to the point. You have made as-
sumptions, and you're clearly not the first, but as a journalist you
ought to know better. The world is different than it was when I
was a professional, so perhaps you, in your modern naïveté, cannot fathom what I am about to explain. When I went with Guy to
the court, I did not "fall behind him as a lowly clerk." What Guy
and I shared professionally was something like perfect symbio-
sis. We worked in symmetry to each other. Our shared work was
almost seamless. Don't mistake what I'm saying; we could argue,
knock down, drag out fights over a case, but neither of us offend-
able, both of us ultimately fixated on the law, without strings. We

savored it, both of us in love with the practice of law (to a fault). Guy and I were equals within the context of our relationship to each other, and I don't know of another woman my age who was afforded that opportunity professionally. In the seventies, when I was really starting out, it was women as secretaries, or if they climbed up from there, some limited scope of what men were doing, and with an ongoing through line of what is now termed sexual harassment at the very best. I didn't have a snowball's chance in hell of my own judicial appointment back then, but I knew what Guy and I had would carry over. You want to know why I forwent prestige and money to become a "lowly clerk"? Because I was not in the practice of law as a means to wealth or fame. Clerking for Guy was not lowly in the least.

I'll leave your closing questions alone—I feel no need to grapple with your youthful idealism. Additionally, you would not be the first person to speculate if my relationship with Guy extended beyond professional. I assure you it did not, and that is something you'll have to accept on my good authority. While we made an exceptional pair in legal contexts, personally we didn't mix. He was, speaking frankly, <u>off the record</u>, rather idiotic socially. He made terrible jokes. He flirted with tall, younger women. He had terrible taste in office furniture, music. He ate like an animal. Honestly, sometimes I couldn't really tolerate him at all. He's lucky he found Liz—that woman is as classic as they come.

There is no need for you to write me again, but I'll close by suggesting you do be careful with your assumptions, Alex.

Regards,

Sybil Stone Van Antwerp

Sybil Vanantwerp
17 Farney Rd.
Arnold, MD 21012

12 Sept. 2012

To: Sybil Vanantwerp, clerk to deceased Judge Guy D. Donnelly

I found the obituary for Judge Donnelly on the internet and an article about you. From time to time I search his name, and this time he died so there is plenty. It says you were "brilliant", and "respected", "Butch and Sundance" like a myth. Says your opinions were "Clean and neat as a pin". This PERFECT JUSTICE. Reading this I felt sick. I remember you. I know you are a cold metal bitch. There is something more important than law and people with their lives do not fit into one box. What you call justice is like an army tank driving through and crushing without mercy, and when it is gone there is only wreckage.

It was easy finding your address, and seeing it on a map. A house near the water, a nice successful life and happy retirement. But I wish you the very worst, it is what you deserve.

Very sincerely,

DM

Ms. Joan Didion
30 E. 71st St. #5A
New York, NY 10021

November 14, 2012

Dear Joan,

Thank you for your letter, which did arrive as you'd intended on the 7th of November. It was very good of you to remember that. You asked how long ago Gilbert had passed away, and this past July it was thirty-nine years. He would have turned nine the November 7 following. Do you know, I had to sit down and do the math again, and that made me feel bad. I feel it's something I should know immediately and it's a bit like disrespect that I don't. Another way of punishing myself for the rest of time.

In response to your second, more complex question, I've sat and thought for nearly a week. How does it all feel to me now?

I suppose there is this one part of it, which is, Gilbert has never left me, and the circumstances of his death have never for one day diminished, and as I age it feels so strange that the majority of people with whom I come in contact don't have the slightest inkling that he ever lived. I had him for so much less time than I've lived without him, and yet his presence is enormous, though I keep it to myself. It is as if I've swallowed a hot air balloon but try not to let on.

There is an articulation of life one hears again and again. People will say, 'oh, this is only a season.' You know what I am referring to, don't you? I mean how if someone is in difficulty they'll say 'it's only a season.' Or if someone is having a new baby and in the sleepless nights, an older woman will comfort with this idea that the expanse of time is a season—a winter, I suppose? (rather, a hurricane season!)—and the season will change eventually to something sunnier. I take issue with this. There are, by definition, four seasons that repeat in measured pattern year after year. As there is no such rhythm in the human life, I have to think that when it comes to seasons we all get one round. We are born and grow through childhood in spring. We live those glorious, lively, interesting years of our twenties, thirties, forties in summer. We settle into ourselves in autumn, that cool but not yet cold time, rich and aromatic. And in winter we age (brutally) and die. One turn of the seasons per person, unless it's cut short, like it was for Gill, and like it was for Quintana Roo. I suppose, on this schedule, we'd say your John had made it to fall. My mother died in her summer.

But I think of life rather like a long road we walk in one direction. By and large a lonesome walk out in the wildness of hills and wind. Mountains. Snow. And sometimes there is someone to come along and walk with you for a stretch, and sometimes (this is what I'm getting to) sometimes you see in the distance some lights and it heartens you, the lone house or maybe a village and you come into the warmth of that stopover and go inside. Maybe you have a warm supper and stay a night or maybe you stay there a few years. I had one of those stopovers when the children were young, just before Gilbert died, and Daan and I were happy, even though I didn't know it was happiness at the time because it felt like busyness and exhaustion and financial stress and self-doubt. But Gilbert's death was a swift ejection back out to the loneliest bitter stretch of road, and that is the bone crunching grief. I'm not saying I've not come in from the wind a few more times in my life; I have. And of course I have my other children, and they have been a joy and comfort. I'd like to say they were enough, but it wasn't enough, and that is another avenue of grief, but anyway my point is I tire of people speaking of seasons as if you can count on three months of winter turning out three months of summer on repeat. It's not so. The stretches on the high, wind-blown road are far commoner than the stopovers in comfort, and aren't we always trying to get back to the happier times? I think that is what it feels like, with Gill. I've spent my life trying to get back to having him even though I know I cannot.

I understand perhaps you are asking how the grief wears over time partly from a place of kindness and partly, on the other hand, from a place of self-preservation, and understandably so, wondering what you should expect in your own situation of hell. Perhaps reading this you would like to think you will fare better than I have fared—and perhaps you will. In any case, I wish I could say after all this time it's easier, but it's not easier. I do have longer stretches, though, when Gilbert doesn't come to mind, and that is a relief, I suppose. This time of year, though, with the trees fully bare and the leaves collecting in drifts, the sky rather endlessly gray, the expanse of now through to the end of the holidays is abhorrent to me. I hold my breath and wait for January. I barely decorate. A few lights in the windows is all I can muster.

Do let me know how you are getting on, with your own life and work, and how you are feeling, your own musings, anything—when you have time. I'll look forward to your next letter—

With very warm regards I write,

Sybil

Dec. 25, 2013

Dear Ms. Van Antwerp,

Merry Christmas. The lights in your windows always bring cheer to the face of your house, and to the street. I hope you are keeping well, and your holidays are enjoyable. I was in Annapolis yesterday and the decorations are lovely, as usual. The lights on the masts of the sailboats.

Please enjoy the caramels with your children, whom I see are in town,

T. Lübeck

January 1, 2013

Dear Mr. Lübeck,

Thank you for the caramels. It's very neighborly of you, year after year, and speaking of years, a new one is upon us and I wish you good health and prosperity.

Regards,

Sybil Van Antwerp

To: Ms. Sybil Van Antwerp
of, 17 Farney Road
Arnold, Maryland
21012
USA

January 5, 2013

Please join the family and close friends of Judge Guy D. Donnelly for a memorial service honoring his life and service to his country on Saturday, February 16, 2013, at the St. John's Church of Frederick, Maryland. The service will commence at 3 pm, with a reception to follow at the family home.

St. John's Church of Frederick
8 Main Street
Frederick, Maryland

Reception at the Donnelly family home
733 Oak Tree Lane
Frederick, Maryland

We hope you are able to join us for this special event,

The Donnelly family, et al.

Sybil, we'll be very glad to see you again, even though it's sorry circumstances. Would you be willing to say a few words at the service? You are so good with words, and you were so special to Guy. It doesn't have to be lengthy—just a little something. With love, Liz

They've scheduled the funeral for Guy at last, and it'll be on February 16, so that's finalized. Liz has asked me to deliver some kind of homily, which has me in a bit of a panic. I ought to simply refuse, but then the woman's husband has just died, so you like to say yes to anything she asks.

The thing is that I have been called upon to speak at a funeral only one other time in my life, and it went poorly. A terrible result. My mother died with cancer when I was eighteen. I wish you could have known her. She was beautiful, kind, patient. She had these two odd duck adopted children and she treated us as if we were the king and queen! She was always sort of laughing, or smiling, or making light. Anyway, she had cancer on again off again through her life, and it killed her eventually, and when it did my father went to pieces. Honestly, it was like my mother was the makeup of his skeletal system, she died and the bones POOF disappeared, and the rest of him, the meat, the organs, the skin, slopped to a pile. He was this way for about a year until he remarried (new bones, new skeleton). Anyway, when Mother died someone had to deliver remarks and I took one look at my father and knew he wouldn't be able to do it, and my brother was young (only ten years old) and he'd gone mute. Felix didn't speak a word from when she died until he was twelve or so (let me tell you, that was an entire situation in and of itself), so I was the one for the eulogy. I wrote something to read, had it all down, just your standard things about how she'd been a good mother, and referencing her kindness in adopting children, etc., and her volunteerism in the community. I got up to the front of the church and I'd been feeling fairly awful that week between her death and the service, just a dull nausea, the way my body was inhabiting the grief, and I stood there, went hot, and vomited. Mortifying.

That said, I do feel it would afford me the opportunity to

answer certain questions that have been asked of me over the years. Explanations for why I would give up the law practice to follow Guy to the courts. Not that the man's funeral should be my platform, but it would be good to have an audience—I've never had the opportunity to talk about how wonderful it was. I do miss it. Anyway, the more I think about it, the more I think it might be a good opportunity to say my piece and close the door. We'll see.

My sight seems to be holding.

TO: jameswlandy@gmail.com
FROM: sybilvanantwerp@aol.com
DATE: Jan 18, 2013 10:26 AM
SUBJECT: Memorial service

Dear James, Were you invited to the funeral? They're finally getting around to it six months later, and by invitation! As if it's the royal wedding. He must be ashes by now, doubt they've kept the old shell on ice for half a year. It's uncouth. It bothers me, it honestly does. Makes me think I need to have a conversation with my own children. Anyway, it gets worse. Liz asked me to speak at the service, SPEAK dear God the horrors never cease, as if getting there wasn't enough a task, so do let me know if you'll attend (if you were invited). If you were not invited, perhaps you could come along as my plus one? I'd rather not drive out to Frederick alone is what I'm getting at, James, and Bruce is taking his children skiing in Colorado. It would be good if you would pick me up.
Do get back to me.

Warm regards,
Sybil

TO: sybilvanantwerp@aol.com
FROM: jameswlandy@gmail.com
DATE: Jan 18, 2013 11:11 AM
SUBJECT: RE: Memorial service

Sybil,

What's ironic is that I hadn't seen Bruce in a while, but we ran into each other last week at a cocktail party at which time he mentioned the ski trip. I did receive an invitation. They couldn't open up the service to the public or announce it in the papers. Think of all the furious people who would take the chance to throw a bucket of pig's blood all over the casket (or urn). I'll be happy to pick you up. Marly won't want to spend a Saturday at a funeral in the country anyway. Although maybe you should take the opportunity to bring an eligible man as your date. What about that guy on your street with the white brick house and the rosebushes? Didn't his wife die a few years ago? God, now this is starting to cross a line.

Of course you have to speak. There's no Butch without Sundance. You're the only man for the job.

I'm changing topics. It's good of you to continue writing letters to Harry. He takes it seriously, in a good way. I worry about him, especially now that his sisters aren't home much. The girls seemed to soothe him. Once he finds his way as an adult I won't worry as much, I guess.

See you in February, and will look forward to your oration—

James

TO: jameswlandy@gmail.com
FROM: sybilvanantwerp@aol.com
DATE: Jan 19, 2013 12:04 PM
SUBJECT: Re: RE: Memorial service

Dear James,

You will never stop worrying.
I don't know how you remember Theodore Lübeck's rosebushes.
(Re: Lübeck, he's from Germany. I asked right out a few weeks back
when he passed on the road—not what I thought—Oregon or Washington or the like. Once he said it, I thought I could detect the accent.)
You ought to let me bring Harry as my plus one.

Warm regards,
Sybil

Rosalie Van Antwerp
33 Orange Lane
Goshen, CT 06756

February 4, 2013

Dear Rosalie,

Fiona called this week to tell me she is pregnant. Apparently it took an awfully long time, a petri dish and more capital than the down payment on a house (it's astounding how much money she makes, not that I know specifically), none of which she chose to share with me until after the fact. She is going to have the baby over there; dual citizenship is a perk. There were some concerns, but now she's well into the second trimester. I suppose this makes you its great aunt or/and the 'godgrandmother.' I'm sure I won't know the child, as I only see Fiona once a year at this point.

In other news, Guy's funeral is two Saturdays hence all the way out in Frederick, so I'll have to go. The last time I was in Frederick was years ago. It is a lovely part of the state, with the big horse farms, but you know how I loathe to drive highways. Anyway, I was going to see if Bruce would come with me, which I'm certain he would have because Bruce positively loved Guy, but I remembered Bruce will be on vacation skiing in Colorado with his children, so I have asked James Landy to drive me. Do you remember James? He came to clerk for Tom Buggs in the late eighties. James is a little uptight, and married to a real wreck of a woman riddled with nerves from a wealthy family out in California or some far-flung place, but I've always liked him and he has a child with whom I correspond. I'm getting into unnecessary weeds here, I'm getting around to this: Liz Donnelly has asked me to speak at the service, and although I do not, like most, relish retracing old paths (better to leave the past in the past where it belongs, if you ask me), I've agreed, so I'll need something to WEAR. I've now stood before my closet on three occasions and leafed through what I own, and the only black anything I have anymore is a dress I was probably wearing in the 1990s, which dips down to the uppermost part of what used to be my cleavage, but which now resembles the skin of a raw plucked chicken. That won't do. I feel I need to present myself with a certain measure of command, some self-respect. I don't think I told you yet, but I've gone fully gray. Fortunately, it's turning out to have a bit of that luxurious shine some women get, and it's smooth, but I do look OLD. Do you have any thoughts on this matter? It was always at these sorts of events when I wished for a bit of height—how I loathe my height—and it's not a miracle I'm asking for! I don't need to be six feet tall like yourself, but five foot five or six would've been nice. Five feet one inch is embarrassing for things like public speaking (which I loathe to begin with) and no self-respecting septuagenarian is going to wear pumps, though I will say I do miss wearing them.

It's been raining for a week straight and the yard is mud. I am reading <u>Murder on the Orient Express</u> (Agatha Christie; third time). What are you reading? Do you hear from Daan?

Sending love, (WRITE TO ME),

Syb

Sybil Van Antwerp
17 Farney Rd.
Arnold, MD
21012

February 8, 2013

Dear Sybil,

How wonderful for Fiona! She texted me just this morning to say she's pregnant. I am happy for you, and the fact that you'll have a grandchild in London means you'll have to visit. This is the perfect opportunity for you to finally GO, take her shopping for baby things and maternity tops, you know, see Buckingham Palace and the very tall clock which has a man's name that escapes me. Put down this letter and call the airline, Sybil!

It's good you can get the funeral out of the way, and lovely Liz asked you to speak. I've always wondered if she resented you at all, how close you were to Guy and all the time you spent with him in those years you were with each other more than you were with your spouses. It's a nice gesture for her to ask. I feel that it shows there isn't any bad feeling. And if you're looking like a chicken, imagine how much worse I am, all the baby oil I bathed in every summer until I was forty. I wish I could come down and take you to Nordstrom and help you find something. You'll think I'm crazy, but I actually sat here considering it, but I can't leave Paul with anyone overnight. He's heavy to get in and out of the bed, and he gets agitated when it's anyone but me. He liked the one day nurse, Olga (she was born in Moscow and lived there until she was eighteen—she was a very interesting person to talk to), and she was willing to do overnights, but she moved to live near her family in Illinois. His new wheelchair is here and it's really something. It has a button for everything, it practically fixes you a cappuccino, although it's extremely heavy.

You asked about Lars. He's getting quieter all the time, and

when he does talk it's almost always nonsense, and then sometimes he comes out with these magnificent statements and that's
like the sun breaking through on a cloudy day. As a matter of
fact, you will get a kick out of this, last week at the breakfast table
I refilled his coffee cup and he touched my arm, looked me right
in the eyes, and said he was thinking of having coffee when we
were on vacation in Bar Harbor in 1964 and I was wearing that
yellow dress and big sunglasses, and there was an orange cat
slinking around the table, and, Sybil, he was exactly right because when he said it, that morning did come back to me, just
like he said, and even the year was right; we'd all five (you had
Bruce, didn't you? I think you were pregnant with Gilbert)—
taken the train up. His face was clear, and it was like it was five
years ago, the old Lars, so I tried to keep him there, but it only
lasted a moment. Between the two of them, I'm exhausted and it
feels lonely, even though I'm with one or both of them all the
time. I certainly did not see this coming—caring for husband
and son as if they were toddlers or less until the end of time.

Listen to me complain. Forgive me.

BIG BEN.

Of course I hear from Daan, but I'm not getting into that now.
Paul's stirring. Please fill me in on Bruce, how his work is going,
etc., the children.

I am reading Crossing to Safety by Wallace Stegner. Did you
already read this? Miss you. My best to dear Bruce. And my best
to Trudy and Millie—

Love, Rosalie

(Oh! Almost forgot to mention: how is Theodore Lübeck? Would
also like an update on your vision if you feel like giving one.)

Sybil Van Antwerp
17 Farney Rd
Arnold MD 21012

Feb 18

Sybil,

It was excellent to finally make the acquaintance of Judge Donnelly's famed work wife. For years I've heard mention of your name, people surprised we didn't know each other. And then to meet you only to find you were there working away behind the scenes when I was representing Evansberg in the Eastern Shore property suit. I guess we were in a revolving door at the same moment in time. I confess I arranged my schedule in order to meet you at the service, and my plan worked. I'd also like to add here that your remarks were very well done, what the career alongside Guy was to you and for you. I was fascinated by your articulation of what drew you to the practice of law. I was moved, and I am rarely moved. It's a wonderfully amusing thing when a woman can deliver a good punch line and keep a straight face.

Now I would give you a call, but I have it on good authority that you are a woman of correspondence (and I am interested to know how it is, or why it is, you have maintained so quaint and impractical a practice), so I've dug out this stationery to write you a letter instead. I will be visiting friends in Baltimore in two months, starting mid-April. Would you please join me for dinner on April 29 at the Capitol House in Annapolis at seven o'clock? It will be good fun to swap stories. I won't take no for an answer—

Mick Watts

478 Chester Place
Houston TX 77055

Sybil Vanantwerp
17 Farney Rd.
Arnold, MD 21012

18 Feb. 2013

To: Sybil Vanantwerp, chief clerk for Judge Guy Donnelly

They buried him. They waited a long time. I bet you were there. I was looking for the details for months and then it was in the newspaper the next day February 16. Do you want to know what I did? I drove all the way to the church four and a half hours from me. It's a big graveyard, but I found him. There was a security guard so I pretended to be paying tribute. The guard turned around to give me privacy, and I spit on it. Guy D. Donnelly FAMILY MAN AND PATRIOT. I spit on the gravestone and I will do the same to yours.

Sincerely,

DM

Liz Donnelly
733 Oak Tree Lane
Frederick, MD 21703

February 18, 2013

Dear Liz,

Hopefully you're settling into life the way it is now without Guy. The service was beautiful with the organ player, and the songs you chose were very appropriate. I thought you looked excellent as well. I wanted to thank you for giving me the opportunity to speak. It was an honor and a gift to me. What Guy and I got to do those years we worked together was special. I think most people spend the workdays watching the clock and living for the weekends, but that wasn't the case for me. There was a lengthy stretch of my life when I lived for the work. It was a haven for me, getting to the office and into the work, and so much of that was because of the partnership with Guy, so thank you for allowing us to have that, Liz. Now that that part of my life is over, I keep it in a box, forgetting that the contents of that box are vast, endless! It's been nice taking the lid off and rummaging around a bit.

Enclosed is a 25% off voucher for Applebee's. Thought you might not be in the mood to cook. On Tuesdays their cocktails are half price.

Warm regards,

Sybil

Mr. Mick Watts
478 Chester Place
Houston, TX 77055

March 13, 2013

Dear Mr. Watts,

Thank you for your invitation to dinner, but 'no' is my answer, and you'll have no choice but to take it. I have alternate engagements on this date. Now that you mention Evansberg, everything falls into place. You should have mentioned the suit at the memorial, and then perhaps I would not have stood staring at you like a glass eyed fish. Of course I remember Evansberg, a two-year plague, and the name M. Watts on every page that came across my desk.

Regarding your remarks on my remarks, firstly, it was a bane to stand up there and speak. Secondly, I don't see that there is anything terribly unique in what drew me (and, in fact, Guy) to the practice of law. The appeal for someone like me (us) to find, on the face of this mad, inside-out, senseless, barbaric, intolerably fraught and painful and mind-spinning planet, some semblance of order . . . well, of course it's appealing. There's nothing quite like the comfort of the law, black and white, other than, perhaps, if you are a religious person, which I am, a religious text, but even the Bible puts one into a wretched state of confusion with all of its doublespeak and nuance, if one really gets into it, though with a religious text one is, of course, suspending all disbelief and throwing caution to the wind.

You also asked after the meaning of my practice of letter writing, calling it quaint and impractical (which was more telling of you, Mr. Watts, than it was offensive to me, though it was, still, offensive to me).

Imagine all that you have said to another, all the commentary you have exchanged with friends over drinks, over the phone with colleagues and distant relatives, all the prattle sent quickly, mindlessly over e-mail, messages typed into your cellular phone, and really, the sum of this interpersonal communication is the substance of your life, relationships being, as we know by now in our old ages, the meat of our lives; but all of that is gone. Vanished! And one day, Mr. Watts, you yourself will be gone. Perhaps if you have children, they will remember you; if you have grandchildren, they, God allowing, may also retain a few fragments of memory including you, but their children will not. They may keep some old photos in a book on a shelf, and perhaps two or three times in a lifetime may turn the page and find your face and think, Ah, yes, doesn't Jimmy resemble this great-great-grandfather Mick, and continue to turn the page, and so that will be what is left of you, nearly erased, in fewer than three generations, and your life, the life you see from the inside, right now, as monumental, will be reduced to the blood in their veins and perhaps, if you are lucky, a distant namesake, a name plucked from the family tree that has come back in vogue after seventy-odd years as fashionable things tend to do and slapped on a newborn baby who will know nothing of YOU.

And yet, if one has committed oneself to the page, the tragedy I've just laid out will not apply. Imagine, the letters one has sent out into the world, the letters received back in turn, are like the pieces of a magnificent puzzle, or, a better metaphor, if dated, the links of a long chain, and even if those links are never put back together, which they will certainly never be, even if they remain for the rest of time dispersed across the earth like the fragile blown seeds of a dying dandelion, isn't there something wonderful in that, to think that a story of one's life is preserved in some way, that this very letter may one day mean something, even if it is a very small thing, to someone?

If all of this amounts to you as nothing more than drivel, then you might also consider a simpler value of the written letter, which is, namely, that reaching out in correspondence is really one of the original forms of civility in the world, the preservation of which has to be of some value we cannot yet see. The WRITTEN WORD, Mr. Watts. The written word in black and white. It is letters. It is books. It is law. It's all the same. I had some notion of this from as far back in my life as I can remember, and I've been writing letters out into the world since I could form a sentence with a pen (age nine).

Now I've gone on longer than I intended. I wish you a nice visit to the East Coast. Regarding the Evansberg suit: that case was terrific fun, you know, for me. It was those sorts of cases, the ones requiring a bit of sleuthing, I loved best.

Regards,

Ms. Sybil Van Antwerp

Postscript: A good punch line is a good punch line regardless if delivered by a man or a woman. You sound like an old fool with comments like that one.

TO: sybilvanantwerp@aol.com
FROM: grandmaalicelivingston@yahoo.com
DATE: Apr 6, 2013 09:40 PM
SUBJECT: <None>

Hello Sybil,

Debbie Banks is furious with you after you stood up to her Thursday, and she's making noise about invoking the third article of the club bylaws, and calling an "emergency vote" to have you overthrown (and me with you, I'm sure). I just got off the phone with her. I sided with you as a matter of friendship, Sybil. I've known you for more than twenty years, but is it worth all of this?

Alice

TO: grandmaalicelivingston@yahoo.com
FROM: sybilvanantwerp@aol.com
DATE: Apr 7, 2013 12:02 PM
SUBJECT: Regarding your e-mail of 9:40 pm last night

This is pure egotistical insanity and I'll not lie down for it. It's a _**garden club**_, for the love of the universe, a gathering of individuals for
the purpose of discussing GARDENING, and Debbie Banks is not
going to dictate the presentation material as a means to boost her
own already-too-puffed-up ego. Why should her son present to us
on matters of real estate? It has nothing to do with gardening whatsoever, and furthermore, I cannot think of a single one among us
who gives a rat's ass about the real estate market. None of us is
moving. Debbie wants to parade her son out like a dog at the American Kennel Club because she thinks he's God's greatest gift to the
world (do you remember how intolerable she was when he got into
business school at Harvard, save me) and I'll tell you a point of fact:
that child has one thought in his little money-grubbing birdbrain, and
that is old rich women and waterfront real estate. Do you know
what? I bet Debbie is in on it! She's no idiot, you know, she had a
prenup before anyone knew what prenups were. She wants him to
charm a bunch of old has-beens like us with his good looks and
make him a bit of money, and she's not doing it at my club. No thank
you. HE WAS FLIRTING WITH MAUDE O'REILLY. Maude is eighty
and she's been smoking two packs a day since 1970, BUT she
owns three acres just on the expensive side of the Naval Academy
Bridge with a view of the steeple—I'm sure I don't need to spell it out
for you, Alice. Shameless. I'm refusing for the sake of the members.
Certainly you can see that. Furthermore, how embarrassingly paltry
of Debbie to discuss "overthrowing" the secretary of a garden club,
why if it isn't Napoleon Bonaparte herself—warm regards,

Sybil

Sybil Van Antwerp
17 Farney Road
Arnold, MD
21012

May 1, 2013

Hi Sybil,

I've enclosed a copy of <u>Blue Nights</u> for you. I look forward to your review, as ever. Your thoughts on life and grief meant a great deal to me. The club of parents who have buried children is a membership I wish I did not own, but the sense of being seen is comforting.

I'm writing down notes here and there. This will amuse you—my nephew wants to make a documentary about me. I'm putting him off.

It seems as though the winter has gone for good and we're into gorgeous New York spring now, all the trees in the parks flowering and the snow melted off. It's my favorite time of year. Winters get harder as I age.

My best to your children,
and yourself, with love,

Joan

May 13, 2013, for delivery May 15, 2013
Mr. Harry Landy
98 Dumbarton St. NW
Washington, DC 20007

May 13, 2013

Dearest Harry,

Your handwriting is improving. Well done. It makes very much of a difference in your letters. Not only are they more easily readable, but they seem more dignified. You are still often switching your i's and your e's, so you need to be careful there.

It is beyond my comprehension the lengths to which children will go in the name of cruelty, and I know you know this, but I want to repeat that when someone(s) treats you poorly, it is a reflection of him or herself and the misery within the heart of them. It doesn't help a bit to hear that when you're young, but later it will. My brother suffered at the hands of sadistic classmates for years. As a matter of fact, I wrote a letter to a child named Nathan Briggs pretending to be the vice president of the United States and threatened to put him in prison if he didn't leave Felix alone—he bought it! Never bothered Felix again. We still laugh about that. And you know, regarding Felix, he endured torment as you do, but he is the smartest, kindest man, and he is HAPPY, and his life has turned out to be magnificent, so you'll push through. It's all you can do. I read an article in the Wall Street Journal about a musical artist who lives by a saying, which is: "F_ck the haters." That is a filthy word; however the sentiment in such forceful simplicity is rather catching.

On the subject of high school. St. Joseph's sounds like a fine school and I'm sure you will do very well there. My son Bruce had friends who attended. I recall it being known for a curriculum in the classical tradition, with the practice of math through the lens of logic rather than lumping maths and sciences together.

Regarding your questions, I'll answer truthfully, but I wonder what has you so inquisitive all of a sudden. I was an English major in college, and a pretty good writer. Not knowing another direction to take that would marry writing with something practical and lucrative, I became a paralegal and after a few years of that, went to law school at the University of Virginia. From law school I went into private practice with that old judge who just died, that was before he was the judge, and then when he became judge I went with him to be his clerk (now that's me breezing over something like 30 years of day-in-day-out work). These days I might have been a judge myself, but back then it wasn't popular for women. Your father, who was very clever at Yale Law and wrote for the law review, came along to clerk for another judge on the bench directly out of law school when I'd already been there fifteen years or more, so I took him (your father) under my wing. There is no good explanation for our enduring friendship other than that your father is a smart, funny individual and he won me over with terrible jokes and sandwiches from a deli a block north of the courthouse. But your father was always destined for a bigger pond, so it wasn't more than a few years before he was clerking in the federal courts, and then in private practice, and then his own judgeship.

You asked where I'm from. I grew up all about Pennsylvania, some in Ohio, and down to Maryland eventually. My mother grew up in Arizona and my father in Maine, and furthermore, I was adopted at fourteen months. As you can see, your simple question does not have a simple answer. I did have three children, as it is in your family, but the second one passed away when he was eight years old. His name was Gilbert. I have a son Bruce, who is a lawyer in Alexandria, and a daughter, Fiona, who is an architect and lives in England, and I have two grandchildren (Hank and Violet) and one on the way next month. I am no longer married, you're correct, but my husband did not die. We divorced. He lives in Bruges, Belgium, where he is from.

Was I like you as a child? I suppose in some ways I probably was, though at my age it's hard to remember much about being a child, and when I was young children weren't really considered so much as they are these days. I remember, like you, I was very much a rule follower, rigid about how things ought to be done. I was also very curious, like you. My curiosity was directed at people. I was very small in stature, and I think smallness fostered in me a sense of wonder as well as trepidation, a trepidation exacerbated by the way my parents kept us rather insulated (afraid to lose us, some psychology about adoptees, perhaps, as well as the mentality that with their money they could build a fortress—oh, many, many things, Harry)—I was quiet and watchful. I remember always finding it odd the way people had of speaking around and around a thing rather than directly to the thing, and I was often punished for insolence and rudeness. I think you have had similar experiences. Of course I can appreciate now what my mother was trying to do, trying to make me into the polite sort of person (especially as a girl) the world expects, indeed the kind of person American civilization is built around, but it didn't stick, and I've never really learned that skill. (I think you are more traditionally polite than I was or am, but perhaps you have been forced into this.) I guess I was considered somewhat odd. I wasn't a cheerful, frivolous little girl interested in dolls and drawing. I was serious and rather grave. Watchful, wary. I was a skeptic. I didn't have many friends. I read a great deal. I was reading all the time. I remember that. And I wrote a great many letters as a child. Writing letters was easier for me than speaking; it still is. Now this is getting long, and I apologize. You've got me thinking back on a time I haven't revisited in quite a while.

Why would you think I'm lonely? I am not. I have you, and

my children and grandchildren, and several friends with whom I keep in correspondence, as well as my church and two wonderful friends in town, Trudy and Millie. I could never be lonely.

I wonder, Harry, are you asking if I am lonely because you are trying to find a way to tell me that you are? Don't worry, dear. You can simply tell me.

With warm regards,

Ms. Van Antwerp

It's a gorgeous day here, the sky that bright, tropical blue and the clouds like cotton balls stretched out. I love it here in spring, my garden bursting with colors, all the work of the year paying off. The hydrangeas attract the bees, and the hummingbirds, and everything is very lively around the house. I've just sealed and stamped a letter to Harry Landy. I believe I've mentioned we write monthly, have for a few years. In his last, he asked if I am lonely! Isn't that interesting. He also wanted to know what I was like before I was a grandmother—my history, my childhood—so I told him a bit, and now I've been sitting here at the desk with my tea cooled, veritably lost in trails of the past.

Did I ever tell you that when I was about nine years old my parents gave me a short letter that had been written by my birth mother when she handed me off? The letter was written to them, not me, but Mother (my adoptive mother) felt I ought to have it. As a child I was tormented by the matter of my adoption. I asked questions about it openly, read books about orphans, imagined an alternative life for myself. I don't know why it is, it isn't as if my parents were cruel or dismissive of me; they were wonderful. I think my parents regretted having told me when they did, though it was so obvious I wasn't related to them biologically. They were both very fair, blond, blue eyes, and me with these dark features and skin several shades deeper; my hair as a child was a thick, glossy black.

I began writing letters and became obsessed. Most often, when I wrote, I got a letter back. This surprises people, but I have found that most people write back. The first letter I ever wrote was in 1948 to P. L. Travers regarding her book <u>Mary Poppins</u>. I loved this book and read it numerous times. I loved that Mary Poppins conducted her own life, and the lives of the children Jane and Michael, in such a controlled, even military, manner. This appealed to me terribly, that level of strict control—it seemed very safe. But also, somehow, there was such a great deal of creativity, adventure, color, surprise! And there was something about—Mary Poppins wasn't their mother, and you knew (even as a child) she couldn't rightly stay there forever, but as a child I imagined this lovely secret, that Mary Poppins was <u>my</u> real mother and that one day she would float down into my yard on the handle of an umbrella and declare I was her daughter, and she would explain the whole reason for having farmed me out, and then she would settle, and take me back and mind me with that perfect combination of wonder and predictability, though I knew obviously the book was a work of fiction and she would not, and also, didn't I know, Colt, that as much as I wanted this, I also didn't want it. I knew the moment she settled in to become the mother I wanted to be mine, that would be the end of the magic. There would be no bottomless bag. There would be no jumping into chalk drawings as portals to other worlds. It's been a long time since I thought back to the business about Mary Poppins. P. L. Travers wrote me back and I have it somewhere here at the house. Anyway, my point is that I was obsessed with letters and I was rather obsessed with the notion of my birth mother, so Mother gave me this letter she had been given at my adoption.

I've just gone and found it. It's a short little note on some flimsy paper. The writing is in blue ink. The penmanship is very slanted, the letters as long and slim as birch trees. I'm going to copy the letter for you. It says:

To: Mr. and Mrs. Stone,

Good day. I hope you will mind my daughter, Sybil, with attention and kindness. She is a quiet and alert baby, and won't give you a bit of trouble. She is only upset by very loud noises and she seems quite terrified of animals, though she is quickly soothed by singing. When she is older, if she knows about me, and if it pleases you, I hope you will tell her she was a perfect baby, born at dawn under a pink sunrise. She has been very dear to me. All my thanks and prayers, most earnestly, L.T.

So that's where this all began. You would think I'd have it down to memory by now, but for some reason the only part that stays word for word in memory is the bit about being born at dawn under a pink sunrise. Isn't that lovely? Makes me miss a thing I never really had.

Now I don't think about it, at least not like I used to—although I do sometimes. Yes, I suppose it's still rather always there, part of the original foundation. There, even if I'm not thinking about it consciously. There it is down at the bottom. But the letter writing stuck to me. I wonder what I will do when I am no longer able to see. I am much too old a dog for the learning of a new trick, like braille or dictation. I suppose, like a fish plucked from the pond and left on a sunbaked dock, I'll probably die.

Emerson Franke, Editor in Chief
The Baltimore Sun
300 East Cromwell Street
Baltimore, MD 21230

TO: The Editor in Chief of the Baltimore Sun
FROM: Sybil Stone Van Antwerp, reader and subscriber for more
       than forty years
DATE: June 10, 2013

Dear Sir or Madam (with a name like Emerson, one can't know which):

SHAME ON YOU. I am writing in regards to the article printed on page 2 of the Life section this morning, June 10, 2013, regarding the death of the young girl in Timonium. It was a disgusting, unfeeling blip that should not have been put in a newspaper at all. What good does it do to print a thing like that, for the gawking of strangers and for the humiliation of that girl's poor father, who is no doubt already nearly killing himself with guilt? Children die regularly—a terrific unfairness—and you don't advertise that. But a man backs over his child with a vehicle—now that's newsworthy. . . . I SPIT upon the unfeeling soul who wrote it. I am repulsed. As if one family's horror is some kind of spectacle the rest of us have right to observe. Let the family print an obituary for the poor child if it's what they choose, but to print a thing like that. To make shark bait of someone's life. Have you no soul within your cold chest? You are clearly not a parent, or if you say the printing was an oversight, then even more shame heaped upon your miserable self for this careless treatment of your post. I have it in mind to cancel my subscription. I know you won't print this, but I hope you read it and I hope it inspires for you, even for the briefest moment, a measure of self-reflection.

TO: The Dean of the College of English
University of Maryland, College Park
College Park, MD 20742

August 10, 2013

Dear Ms. Genet,

Congratulations on your recent appointment to the deanship of the College of English. I have enjoyed infrequent communications with your most recent predecessors. A little over ten years ago when I retired, I contacted Dick Wright to ask after the possibility of auditing a literature course. He was gracious to welcome me to campus, and I sat for EN305 South Asian Literature. It was tremendous, my first foray into Salman Rushdie and his <u>Satanic Verses</u>. In the following years, I have audited a variety of courses (Seventeenth-Century British Poetry; Irish Literature; South Asian Literature; Eighteenth-, Nineteenth-, and Twentieth-Century American Literature; and others), and after Dick came Henry Dougherty, who also welcomed me. I missed the chance to register the last two summers, but I would be loath to miss another autumn. I am writing to request the course list and schedule for the fall. Please let me know if there are certain courses you think might be a better fit than others. I am unable to attend evening classes, as I have to drive to and from my home just outside Annapolis, and additionally I would rather avoid poetry, if at all possible. I find poetry terrifically dull. The last time I registered, the fee for auditing was $250. If the fee has gone up, do advise. Otherwise, I will send the check. You can write back by mail, or my e-mail address is: SYBILVANANTWERP@AOL.COM.

Warm regards,

Sybil Van Antwerp

Sybil Van Antwerp
17 Farney Rd.
Arnold, MD
21012

September 25, 2013

Dear Sybil,

It's late, but I can't sleep. I have the window open and the wind chimes you gave me several birthdays ago are wind chiming. Daan called tonight, and I went back and forth if I would write or call. If it were me I guess I would want you to be the one to tell me. He's been diagnosed with colon cancer that's already spread up into his intestine and stomach. They're going to be starting with treatments and he'll have a surgery for discovery later this week to see how far it's progressed. He sounded like the same old Daan, calm and optimistic. He said Lina is very upset (of course she is). I know I'm not supposed to, but I feel sorry for her. He told Fiona and Bruce yesterday, but asked them not to tell you immediately. He thought maybe he should call you, but I said I would let you know. I'm not sure how this will feel to you. I'm sorry, Syb. Don't be angry with Fiona and Bruce, you know they're caught in the middle and they're always trying to do their best by both of you.

I tried explaining the news to Lars. Daan had already been on the line with him for a while. It's sweet the way Daan talks to him about the past. I guess history is all they have anymore. Daan will say something like, Remember when we took the train with Mother to see her sister in France . . . and go on into some old memory like he's telling a story to a child. Lars seems to listen. He certainly recognizes Daan's voice, you can see the way it calms him. After Daan had been talking to Lars for a while I took the phone off speaker and Daan told me about the cancer, so after we hung up I tried telling Lars. I can't tell if any of it got through to him, but then I got to thinking what's the point in making sure Lars understands? Maybe it's better if he doesn't. I brought out a photo of them from our wedding, wondering if seeing a younger version of his brother might jostle his mind to remembering a bit. I hadn't looked at those photographs in years! They really did look like twins, didn't they? I have no idea what Lars did or didn't understand, but he held the photo for a long time staring at it, breaking my heart.

Anyway, I know it's somewhat crass to put the two side by side in a letter, but I'm thinking about the man from Texas you said has written twice to ask you to dinner, the one you met at the memorial service, and you keep pushing him off. The fact that he wrote again after your first (harsh) reply, and sent those flowers as an apology, says something about him (something lovely). What harm would it do to go to dinner? I worry about you.

I'm reading Never Let Me Go by Kazuo Ishiguro. It's very dark. What are you reading? Give me a call when you get this letter if you want to.

Love,

Rosalie

(How is Fiona doing with the baby? Did she like the blanket you sent? Is she calling him Charles or Charlie?)

Ms. Van Antwerp
17 Farney Road
Arnold, MD
21012

October 2, 2013

Dear Ms. Van Antwerp,

I am writing in response to your two letters (dated August 10 and August 25) in which you requested permission to audit a literature course in the University of Maryland College Park College of English, undergraduate. I regret to inform you that I am unable to extend this permission. Courses at the University of Maryland are reserved exclusively for students enrolled at the college, and we have made changes to certain regulations, including the loophole that was employed to allow your audit of many courses in the past.

Sincerely,

Melissa Genet

Dean of the English Department

Professor of Poetry/Poetry Workshop

Undergraduate and Graduate

University of Maryland, College Park

College Park, MD

Dec. 25, 2013

Dear Ms. Van Antwerp,

Merry Christmas. I see your children are in town. Here are some cookies I thought you might all enjoy. Also enclosing an article I saw in this morning's Times about the Christmas markets in Germany in the town where I was born. When I was a child Christmas was a spectacle, but nothing like it is now.

No need to return the tin. I find they are useful for storage of things like buttons or bolts when the cookies are gone. In addition, I noticed you've changed your hair. It's very elegant.

Your neighbor,

T. Lübeck

Felix Stone
7 Rue de la Papillon
84220 Gordes
FRANCE

December 27, 2013

Dear Felix,

Well, I must know: Did Stewart cook a Christmas goose for your first as a full-time citizen? All I can think of is that great hollow gong of a voice coming from Julia Child on the television:

BON APPÉTIT

Haven't my gifts arrived yet? Damn the Federal Express. One should always go with the United States Postal Service, you know, it's an institution as faithful and true as an old hound. The Federal Express ran their holiday special and I took the bait, and here I am paying the pied piper, though I probably ought to blame French customs, blasé and uninterested in expediency. If you haven't gotten them, here's spoiling. I sent two dress shirts, a pair of corduroys, and a tie with little hens from Nordstrom for Stewart, and for you it was a first edition of <u>Ulysses</u> by James Joyce, which I found in a collectors bookstore in Annapolis several months ago when I was out to lunch with the birds (Trudy spotted it), as well as a new box of the good Smythson letter writing paper, envelopes, and a fountain pen. This is the way I will prevent you from ever moving our ongoing exchange to e-mail.

The children have all left this morning and I spent the day putting everything back to right. It was lovely. I wish you could have been here. The baby, Charles, is terribly skinny but good tempered, and Bruce's kids (who asked me for cash in lieu of gifts) couldn't keep away from him. Fiona does seem happy, if also thin—maybe it's not that everyone is thin; maybe I'm getting fat—and I was in the kitchen with herself and Marie and we were drinking wine and making the big dinner, and Walt and Bruce out putting toys together and overseeing the children. I guess I rather told you most of this on the phone on the day, but it was the kind of moment that makes one grateful. Anyway, it was a nice Christmas having what remains of my family all in one place. Fiona didn't pick at a single stitch.

Do you know about a website business called Kindred Project? This program will assist a person with uncovering his ethnicity through DNA TESTING. You can also use the program to investigate the network of all people who are using the program to make familial connections. Bruce gave this to me for my Christmas gift. It was a strange moment. Felix, do you have moments when you feel, I don't know, like Pluto way out there on its own, rather observing the workings of the galaxy from a distance? This sense has come to me at odd times throughout my life and I've always attributed it to having been adopted. Does this affect you? I suppose Mother and Dad knew less about my birth situation than yours—and I know you expended a great deal of effort to find information about your birth family, an effort you felt compelled to put forth because of the complexities of that whole situation—but I am not like you. I have been content. (Of course it occurs to me from time to time, at odd times really, like a little bruise, <u>why</u> would someone give up a child? A newborn I can certainly understand. A thing someone decided before the notion of a baby became an actual baby. But a child of fourteen months, what could possess a person to do that? These are thoughts I've had, but not in an urgent sense, just a little bruise I'd press on every once in a while.)

When I opened the gift from Bruce everyone was staring at me, quiet, as if I were on a stage under a spotlight and on display. I was humiliated! Imagining the discussions going on behind my back, them talking about it beforehand. And do you know, I was angry at Bruce for this. Bruce is like me. I have always felt we had a certain understanding. What was he thinking? They were all rather smiling, and Fiona, who hasn't shown a speck of interest in me in a decade (I almost wonder if it was Fiona's idea; it seems like something Fiona would concoct), was going on about finding out a bit about where I came from, as if I am an alien life form. I came from the planet Earth! Perhaps they want to know, for their own sakes, now with their father at death's door. Sentimentality? Half Belgian elite, half WHO THE HELL KNOWS, PROBABLY TRAILER TRASH. I'm embarrassed to admit this, but I was doing my best to hold back tears. I was angry, on display like a fool! I'm very close to the end of my life, Felix, almost there, and I don't want to muck it up more than I already have. It was presumptuous of them to assume I would want to know. I do not want to know. I am perfectly content.

Before I conclude, I wanted to update you on another matter, which is that my hair has fully grown into its natural state, and surprise of a lifetime, it looks elegant.

That is all. I'm angry, as much is clear, but it is as ever, with love, and the warmest regards for a happy and healthy new year, your loving sister,

Syb

December 27, 2013

Dear Mr. Lübeck,

Thank you for the cookies. Happy New Year.

Regards,

Sybil Van Antwerp

Sybil Vanantwerp
17 Farney Rd.
Arnold, MD 21012

20 January 2014

TO: Sybil Vanantwerp, former clerk to Judge Guy D. Donnelly

I imagine you reading my notes standing at the mailbox, heat growing on your neck and the sick feeling in your stomach. Or standing in your kitchen while the water whistled for tea and you didn't hear it because you were distracted by that bad feeling. Or in a chair, I think maybe you squirmed as the meaning in my message became clear to you. I was pleased by that, but it was not enough. I went for a long drive again and I found your blue house with the steep roof and the mailbox like a fish, the bird bath. I sat outside in my car for some time. You have a nice house. It is probably worth a lot of money with the way you can see the river, even though part of your fence is falling. I can tell you are a good gardener, even though it's winter. I am a gardener. I can see everything is organized and trimmed back. You know what you're doing with it. I will come have a look in spring and maybe again in summer, and I hope you think of me outside your house and it disturbs you. I hope it poisons your days and you look out the window the times you feel chilled. I hope you have to look twice, and that little fear keeps you from enjoying the life you have left, in the same way that you impeded me.

Sincerely,

DM

Dear Mr. Lübeck,

This piece of mail was delivered to my house erroneously.

Regards,

Sybil Van Antwerp

Postscript: Have you seen anything odd around Farney Road lately? Anything untoward?

Feb. 5, 2014

Dear Ms. Van Antwerp,

Thank you for bringing down the mail. Why do you ask if I've seen anything troubling on the street? I assume you have. Please do not hesitate to ask me for help with anything at all. If you would like to discuss a matter, you are very welcome to come by for a cup of coffee.

I have noticed you aren't going out as much. Is there a problem with your new vehicle? You would be more than welcome to come along with me to the shops, the post office, the YMCA any time I am going out.

Your neighbor,

Theodore Lübeck

Sybil Van Antwerp
17 Farney Rd
Arnold, MD 21012

March 1

Dear Sybil,

You are stubborn, but I am a patient and persistent man. I will be back on the East Coast in April. Is there any chance of us meeting up then? If it's my quality of character you're unsure about, trust the judgment of the Donnelly family!

Here is my story, in short. I grew up in Wisconsin, but my family moved to Texas when I was 15 for my father's work. He was a laborer, but through mutual contacts was connected to a wealthy ranch owner who was seeking a grounds and estate keeper and manager, and my father took the position. I went to college in Dallas, where I met my first wife, Wendy. We had one child together (my son, Amos) before she divorced me. I married again, too quickly I admit, but we did not have any children together because she didn't want children (turned out that was a good plan), and we divorced several years ago. I've been happily on my own since.

In the last few years, I have found that I miss that ongoing conversation, the idle back and forth to pass in the morning, or while you walk from the car to the restaurant, or whatever it is. I love to travel, but it's not much fun alone. I've tried dating, but good conversation is astonishingly difficult to come by. I retired a few years ago. I was gunning for retirement for my whole career, and then I did it, and at the end, damn it, I find myself bored! Terrifically bored. That is, I was feeling bored until you livened things up. For years Liz Donnelly has dropped your name to me. We're the same age, you and I, I think. I'm 76. There, now we're better acquainted.

I have gone to lengths to apologize for all levels of my malfeasance, and my contrition was, and is, genuine. Now come to dinner with me, Sybil.

Mick

Ms. Joan Didion
30 E. 71st St. #5A
New York, NY 10021

March 5, 2014

Dear Joan,

Well, here I am coming to you with my tail between my legs, unable to bring myself to read <u>Blue Nights</u>. For months it sat there on my desk in the small stack beside my mug of pens. I would finish a book and know yours was there to be started, but I never could, and instead I would take the one beneath it. Seeing the cover began to fill me with dread. It seems where you have found the courage to explore your feelings to the uttermost through writing on the death of your child, I have not. I cannot bear it. I've placed the book in a box in the linen closet at last. Perhaps one day I will have the guts to read it. Please forgive me.

My ex-husband (his name is Daan, he's Belgian) is dying with cancer. We divorced nearly thirty years ago, and with our children grown we have no cause to maintain regular contact. However, there's a strange loophole, and that is my best friend Rosalie is married to Daan's brother, so I do hear things from time to time. It was Rosalie who told me about the cancer. I know cancer, at my age, is inevitable, if not for myself then for someone else, or many others, around me, but even still, hearing this news of Daan has disturbed me.

I hope you don't mind if I get a bit of this down on the page. (I know you don't, Joan.) We had a good marriage. Daan is a gentle, intelligent man. His soft nature is the opposite of mine, but we balanced one another and we shared a great deal in the realm of our thoughts. He was an avid reader of all things and we used to sit up nights just chatting on. He loved to read nonfiction on the history of Europe. He was born into an offshoot of some old line of Dutch aristocracy, raised in Belgium, and he did coursework in history up to the PhD level, though he never finished once the worst happened. He was a high school teacher (one of the only people I've ever met who always, without fail, places a comma correctly—EVERY TIME—and English is his third language) and he did some translating, although with his intelligence I always thought he could have been much more. When Gill died I went very far inside myself, and I suppose Daan was doing the same thing, though it was Daan who continued to raise the remaining children, while I rather disappeared from the family for some time. I took a brief leave from work and I guess it was a few weeks that I stayed in my bedroom, only leaving if everyone was gone and then I would come out like a thief, listening to be sure I was alone and what I would do is go sit in the dirt in the garden with my back against the siding. It was a sweltering summer, but I would sit there for hours. Watching insects, watching the flowers grow—really! I remember scraping my fingers through the soil and the black pushing beneath my nails, in my cuticles, embedded in my fingerprints, fetid, unwashed, sweaty, and staying. And then, you know, after some time of this behavior my nature clicked back on. The garden sitting was a kind of escape or a kind of penance I was making and I didn't deserve either, so I stopped and got back to our life. I went back to work—it was premature, a mistake I see in hindsight, but work was the thing I knew I could do. Something from that time is coming back to haunt me now, as a matter of fact, literally.

When I play it all back I am ashamed, and yet I cannot imagine having done any other thing. Grief shared, I think, can produce two outcomes. Either you bind yourselves together and hold on for dear life, or you let go and up goes a wall too high to be crossed. For us it was the latter.

We kept it going until the children were in high school, but then they were involved in their own lives and out in the evenings, so I started to stay later and later at the courthouse. I used work as an excuse. The research, finding answers to every problem, no matter how convoluted, the making sense of it and writing it all out into a sensical and watertight opinion. When my father died we'd received a substantial payout from his estate and I could have cut back, but the work became my haven from what waited for me at home. I'm sure Daan assumed I was with other men. I wasn't, but I didn't go to pains to convince him. I was sabotaging us. I wanted it to be over. It was so painful, you see, because Daan was—the children, he was Gill, they were all tied up together. I couldn't cut myself away from Bruce and Fiona, but I could cut the stay to Daan, and I did. I knew exactly what I was doing.

I came home one evening when Bruce was away at college and Fiona was out and Daan was in the kitchen. He had opened a bottle of a good wine we kept in the pantry for dinners with friends, and when I walked in and saw him at the counter with the wine, a glass poured for me, I knew. He said he was going to move back to Belgium. I didn't argue. He never liked America anyway. We drank the wine. We had sex, and it was the first time since Gill had died that I wanted to. That was the end of that. A while later he left and Fiona went with him and finished out high school there. I still loved him, I suppose. I just couldn't bear him.

You get the one life. It's awfully unfair, isn't it?

With love,

Sybil

Postscript: Seems to be an individual with an old grudge related to my former work coming back to have it out with me. Writing me notes, just a bit creepy, you know. I'll take precautions, so not to worry.

May 30, 2014

Dear Mr. Lübeck,

Thank you for the roses on my birthday. I don't know how it is
that you know my birthday, and I certainly don't know yours. It
seems it's time I ask, as this is becoming embarrassing.

Warm regards,

Sybil Van Antwerp

June 1, 2014

Dear Ms. Van Antwerp,

I was pleased to meet your friend Millie Wednesday last when she was arriving at your house for a dinner party. I know your birthday is May 29 because years ago your son Bruce arrived carrying a big bunch of sunflowers and a cake. The date holds meaning for me as well, so it's been automatic to remember. I have very few people with whom to share my roses, but if you'd rather not receive them, please tell me, and I won't send any more.

Please do feel free to address me as Theodore, in writing as well as when we see each other on the road. There's no need for me to share my birthday as I would hate for you to have a sense of obligation to send me roses. I have plenty.

Please let me know if there is anything at all you need.

Theodore Lübeck

June 1, 2014

Postcard from Portugal

Sybil Van Antwerp
17 Farney Rd.
Arnold, MD 21012
USA

Syb: I'm coming for a week. Landing in Baltimore on July 1 at 3 p.m. Coming from France. Stewart isn't coming because he has things going on, engagements with people and his cooking courses, but I'm coming because you are scaring me with your miserable crotchetiness. We will spruce things up at the house, go shopping for clothes, talk about the man courting you, and this whole Kindred issue in person. Would love to see Bruce + schedule dinner with Trudy&Millie, too. Please someplace waterside with good crabcakes, maybe the Back Porch Café in Eastport. XX—Felix

TO: customerservice@kindredproject.org
FROM: sybilvanantwerp@aol.com
DATE: Jul 5, 2014 05:22 PM
SUBJECT: PROBLEMS (Attn: Basam)

Hello Basam, You were very helpful on the phone. Typically speaking with customer service agents somewhere over in India is EXCRUCIATING. You answered all the questions I had and now I have follow-up questions.

1. What happens to my DNA after you run it? Is it returned to me or do you dispose of it? I assume it won't be kept, but I'd like assurance.

2. How can I be certain, if I don't check the box for allowing other users to connect to me, that you won't override my choice and share it anyway?

3. Do you have some kind of emergency contact record? If I should die in the midst of this, with my personal information including my DNA off in the cyber world, would you be able to send the information to my brother? Please note his name is FELIX WHITNEY STONE, but we are not biologically related. I can provide you with his phone number and address if it's helpful.

4. If I decide not to go through with it, can you please send the refund to my son, Bruce Van Antwerp, the idiot who purchased this elaborate system of torture for me as a Christmas gift.

I look forward to your response,
Sybil Van Antwerp (Stone, by adoption)

Postscript: I found your English to be quite passable, a cut above what you usually hear from foreigners, so crack on wherever it is you are over in the east.

TO: sybilvanantwerp@aol.com
FROM: customerservice@kindredproject.org
DATE: Jul 7, 2014 11:57 AM
SUBJECT: RE: PROBLEMS (Attn: Basam)

Dear Ms. Van Antwerp,

I do not live in India and I am not Indian. I have lived here in California with my wife and two children for three years. I moved to the US from Syria when my home was destroyed. I have an advanced degree in engineering, but I work at the moment in customer service for Kindred out of necessity because my degree is not enough to prove me in this country.

The laboratory will dispose of your DNA.

I suppose you will have to trust that Kindred Project will abide by the terms of the contract you will sign and follow the directives you will have the choice to set.

I suggest telling your brother your plans to embark on the program and give him your account password so at the point of your death he has no trouble accessing your profile.

Unfortunately, the window for refunds has passed. Bruce would have had to request a refund within sixty (60) days of purchase. His date of purchase was December 23, 2011.

Please don't hesitate to reach out with additional questions! Thank you for contacting Kindredproject.org.

Basam

Mick Watts
478 Chester Place
Houston, TX 77055

July 21, 2014

Dear Mick,

The ultimatum you put down in your most recent letter (dated June 4) was bold. Furthermore, at seventy-six you are quite a bit older than me.

In your letter from March you mentioned the matter of your boredom. Of course you are bored. The mind was not created for idleness. Golf, drinking, staying in one's pajamas until late in the morning, stretching oneself to find ways in which to pass the days is the way we were meant to spend our vacation weeks, not decades of our lives. Guy and I heard a case years back in which a respected physician who retired at the age of sixty-two had, within two years, wrapped himself up in a scheme related to prostitution in Cleveland, been busted and lost all of his money.

That said, early retirement has been wonderful for me.

I will go to dinner with you when you are here in late August because it seems you are rather prepared to continue to ask until the end of your days, or mine. However, the restaurant you suggested, Capitol House, is a stuck-up establishment riding on the coattails of a bygone reputation for good steaks frequented by tourists reading outdated guidebooks and high school students before prom. I'll meet you at Harry Browne's on August 31 at 6:00 pm sharp. I won't stay past 8:00 because I don't drive in the dark.

Regards,

Sybil Van Antwerp

The College of English
University of Maryland, College Park
College Park, MD 20742

TO: Melissa Genet, Dean of the College of English
FROM: Sybil Van Antwerp, woman seeking permission to audit
       course at UMDCP

July 21, 2014

Dear Melissa,

I am writing again to request you reconsider your position on my auditing courses in the UMDCP College of English, something I have done on <u>nine</u> previous occasions with the enthusiastic support of your predecessors. Might I add that since the genesis of my participation in the life of your university in this way I have given generous donations to the College of English every calendar year, as well as paid the auditing fee without gripe despite the fact that my presence in the classroom is of zero consequence? I do not participate (unless called upon). The professors do not grade my work. I might as well be a janitor, or a mouse!

According to the office of the registrar, per the information my son dug up for me on the webpage, UMDCP does, in fact, maintain the allowance of citizens not enrolled in the university to audit courses <u>with the permission of the dean of the particular college</u>. It appears the matter is not one of policy, but of your caprice. Despite this chilly correspondence I would again like to request permission to audit a literature course.

I imagine you to be a reasonable woman. I look forward to your reply.

Ms. Van Antwerp
17 Farney Rd.
Arnold, MD
21012

August 1, 2014

Dear Ms. Van Antwerp,

I'm sorry I didn't write to you on July 1. We were on vacation in Alaska with my sisters and I didn't realize what day it was. When I saw that I missed July I thought it would be better to wait until the next first of the month rather than change the pattern of our letters. How is your eyesight doing? Have you told your brother or your kids you're going blind? How will you live alone when you're blind? Will you learn to read braille? I started to learn, in case you need me to. It's very simple and I think I've mostly got it down. My mother listens to books on CD. You can get them at the library, and there is also a trading program at Cracker Barrel, the roadside restaurant. You can also buy them, but they are <u>extremely</u> expensive.

Here is what happened in June and July:

1. We went on a cruise to Alaska with my sisters. Lauren has a boyfriend and he came. His name is Steve and I don't like him at all because he only talks about professional football and his job in marketing. My dad pretends to care, but I know he doesn't because Dad doesn't watch sports. I liked seeing all the animals (I saw a bear eating salmon in the wild) and being outside. I liked how cool it was in summer, and the landscape was simple, which made me feel really peaceful. I didn't like sleeping in the boat, and there were three nights when I had freakouts and didn't sleep at all.

2. I wrote a story about a made-up world. It is 46 pages single-spaced size 12 Times New Roman font with one inch margins.

3. My mom spent a week in a hospital for people with mental problems and I didn't see her during that time. I have no idea why she went to the hospital. My dad said she is very tired, but she doesn't look tired. He looks tired, actually. I know nobody goes to a mental hospital because they're tired, so I'm trying to figure out what's wrong with her, but Lauren called me and told me it is hard for my dad when I ask loads of questions, so I haven't. This happened in the beginning of June, before Alaska.

4. I went to two weeks of summer camp. The camp was a sleepaway camp and the subject was electrics and engineering, which I like OK. The daytime at camp was good. We did a lot of interesting projects, not stupid stuff, but things with electricity and real tools. We built a model hotel with a working elevator. At night it was pretty bad. I didn't sleep well there. I think I don't sleep well unless I'm at my own house, and Dr. Oliver said that's part of it, but I'm not sure what he means by that. There were some other weird kids like me, but I got made fun of a lot. One morning I put my shoes on and they were wet. I smelled urine, so I knew what had happened. I tried to dry them out with the hand dryer in the bathroom, but that took a long time, so then I missed breakfast, and then I was trying to eat some cereal in the dining hall quickly, but it made me late to one of our sessions so I didn't get to pick my partner, so then I had a freakout. I hadn't had one the whole time, but then I did, so the rest of the time I knew everyone was looking at me and if they hadn't

already known I was weird, now they did. That made me feel embarrassed. I know you will tell me I should tell my parents, but I am not going to. By the way, this whole paragraph is a stone.

My birthday is August 10, which you know, and I'll be 14. Instead of having a party, my dad is going to take the day off and give me an iPhone, take me to the Spy Museum and then for cheeseburgers for dinner. I go back to school on Monday, August 25, which I dread.

Warm regards,

Harry Landy

Kazuo Ishiguro

% Peter Straus / RCW Literary Agency

20 Powis Mews

London W11 1JN

UNITED KINGDOM

August 6, 2014

Dear Mr. Ishiguro,

Please let me begin by expressing my condolences over the unexpected loss of your literary agent, Ms. Rogers.

The primary subject for this correspondence is the matter of your novel, <u>Never Let Me Go</u>, which was recommended to me by a trusted source. I've only finished it last night. I thought it echoed a bit of your earlier novel, <u>The Remains of the Day</u>, which I also read and, you might recall from my letter those years ago, enjoyed very much. You responded to my letter then—much appreciated—though I don't expect you would remember as I'm sure you are inundated with correspondence from readers. But while we're on it, I liked <u>The Remains of the Day</u> better than this book. I related so much to the butler, though his name escapes me now. Perhaps it's time I read it again. The two books do, of course, share certain themes universal to the human experience—isolation, loneliness. It makes me wonder about the pain you have obviously suffered in your life. They also share that similar English countryside locality, and I like that. During the course of reading both books, I felt an urgent desire to visit England (which I will never do, although, never having visited, I imagine living in the English countryside would suit my nature very well).

I ought to get to the point. I'm writing to tell you what I thought about this new book. The story was strange indeed, and it took me at least half the book to really sort out what was afoot at Hailsham because it isn't written like science fiction! How clever. I very much liked the progression of the friendship between Ruth and Kathy. I also marveled at the very direct way in which the story is narrated, and I have spent a bit of time pondering this. You do very well with inhabiting your narrators and telling the story as they would. Of course, the material of this novel is grotesque and terrifying. Do you think one day science will allow for cloning? I suppose it's ridiculous to ask, as you're a novelist and not a scientific researcher, though presumably you did research the topic. In any case, at my old age it's too much to consider and I do hope I'm dead long before it comes to that! (which I will certainly be—it can't be long now) Indeed, I thought it was all very clever, and there were funny parts, and I did cry a few times. You are a very good storyteller and your writing is exquisite, which of course you know, as you have won numerous literary prizes. (A hearty congratulations to you, as well, for being awarded the French Order of Arts and Letters. Bravo.)

If you have any advice for a young aspiring writer, please pass it along. I have a high school aged friend writing bits of fiction and he's rather unhappy. It would be lovely if I could offer him something to cheer him up.

> I look forward to your next
> installment, and it is with
> warm regards I write,
>
> Sybil Van Antwerp

Sybil,

Dinner Friday was great fun. Haven't laughed that hard in ages—
I know you didn't want to have fun, but you did, so let's do it
again. I'm in the area for two more weeks. Meet me again,

Mick

Rosalie Van Antwerp
33 Orange Lane
Goshen, CT 06756

September 8, 2014

Dear Rosalie,

I RAN OVER THEODORE LÜBECK'S CAT WITH MY CAR. OH MY GOD. I was coming in from the garden club meeting this evening around six-thirty. I'd gone to the meeting, and it's as contentious as you can imagine, and then to the Safeway for a few things, and I was coming down the road with the evening sun blinding me through the tree limbs and I had stopped the car in the middle of the street because there was a deer with her two fawns and at first it startled me. Lübeck's cat (it's a slate gray color with white paws) must have come underneath my car, stupid imbecile, while I was stopped and I didn't see it—how could I have? Dear GOD. When the deer darted off into the trees I punched the gas to get going into the driveway and there was a good thwump (I was flummoxed). I stopped again, looked in the rearview and there was a twitching heap I couldn't discern; I got out, it's the CAT in the road! You know, I have no feelings for animals, but oh, Lord, that cat was making a terrible whine and seizing, so I stood there gaping. HORRIFIED. This cat does go outside and it comes around my garden and porch, so I'm always shooing it off. Well, I've shooed it off for the last time. Mr. Lübeck must have seen me from his window stopped in the road because he came out and looked at me, and then he came closer down his walk, saw the cat, and he started saying, "Oh. Oh." I was apologizing and explaining myself and he came over and knelt down by the cat and put his big knotty hand right on the bloody, filthy fur. He asked me to go get a towel. Of course I was not going to bring out one of my own good towels, so off I went, straight in the front door of his house, Rosalie! Just waltzed right in, never set foot inside the man's house before in my life (more on the house to follow), and I went to the bathroom and took a towel from the rack and brought it to him. These were not towels of exceptionally high quality, and a horrible mauve color, and I did take all of this into consideration, but knowing I am able to get bloodstains out of fabrics using peroxide and cold water, I figured what the hell. When I came back out the cat was fully deceased and Mr. Lübeck was on his knees. His old knees in the middle of the street wearing good khaki pants and I could see the top of his head (have I ever told you he is quite tall? A big man, built for sport, like Lars. He still has a good head of white hair). He wrapped the cat in the towel and managed to stand up carrying the cat, and that did impress me, that his knees still work so well. He thanked me for helping him—thanked me! I killed the creature!—and took the cat inside. I stood in the road for a moment. My car was still running just a few paces up toward my house and the deer were gone. Wind in the trees. A gorgeous night. Stain of cat guts on the road.

Regarding Lübeck's house: it was neat as a pin, a mug of coffee steaming beside his La-Z-Boy, a few library books, and I wasn't snooping, but one can't help but notice certain things. It was spartan and tidy, but there were these little things I noticed. There is an old black-and-white photo framed on a table in his entryway of a gorgeous woman with dark hair and eyebrows maybe circa 1920s. His mother, perhaps? He has a few nice pieces of art on the walls, and the furniture is positively threadbare. A photograph beside the recliner of himself and the late wife. In the photo he looks like he'd be about the age Bruce is now. I tell you, though, going inside his house, seeing his few things, it made me feel sad, Rosalie. Boy, I'm wiped.

Syb

Postscript: God almighty, you can see I'm in a state. I am reading The Orphan Master's Son by Adam Johnson. What are you reading?

Second postscript: Mick Watts wants to take me to dinner again—he delivered a note by hand last week. Of course Mick is a bit of an ass. He eats terribly, smokes, and drinks dark spirits, and he's not a reader of fiction . . . but he is funny. God, he's very funny, makes me laugh. Trudy and Millie think I should go again, but they never knew Daan. What do you think?

TO: sybilvanantwerp@aol.com
FROM: jameswlandy@gmail.com
DATE: Oct 22, 2014 11:11 AM
SUBJECT: HARRY RAN AWAY

Sybil, I tried to call you. Your voicemail is full. Harry ran away. He took the golden retriever and a backpack and left around ten this morning. Is he with you? Call my cell.

TO: jameswlandy@gmail.com
FROM: sybilvanantwerp@aol.com
DATE: Oct 22, 2014 10:59 PM
SUBJECT: He is here

James I'm firing this off Harry said if I picked up the phone to call you he would walk right out the door again so I told him I needed to use the bathroom and snuck to computer . He walked all the way here it took him until 10:30PM fortunately was dressed warmly with good shoe ss. He seems very tired but watchful and his pupils are dilated and isn't saying much. I have given him a bowl of chili and cookies I had in a tin and I'll get him to take a shower he's filthy I have no idea what routed he took but I have himself and Thor and you can come collect them in the morning Fr now let's let them sleep Please Do Not call or he will know I'v contacted you and leave again I think he means it Sybi

TO: jameswlandy@gmail.com
FROM: sybilvanantwerp@aol.com
DATE: Oct 24, 2014 9:14 AM
SUBJECT: Security cameras

Hi James, In the midst of Harry's great escape you mentioned you have security cameras on your porch. I went into town to the hardware store but did not see anything of this nature for sale. Please send instructions on how or where to have security cameras installed on one's porch.

I hope things have calmed down somewhat.

Warm regards,
Sybil

December 15, 2014

Postcard from Belgium

Sybil Van Antwerp
17 Farney Rd.
Arnold, MD 21012
USA

Hi from Belgium, Mom. Thought of you today—in a bookshop found a translation of <u>84 Charing Cross Road</u> (Helene Hanff)—did you ever read it? I picked it up and read a few of the letters—forgot how funny they are, reminds me of you a bit. Anyway, bought this postcard there and now sitting having a coffee. The picture is really how it looks here all decked for Christmas, houses like iced gingerbread and lights like candies. Really beautiful. You know I'm not one to write, much easier to pick up the phone and call or text, but I know you love it. Dad is doing OK, pleasant as usual, but thin and quieter, or tired. Will miss you at the holiday—was sweet of you to send the sweater for Charles. Don't be lonely—what are Trudy and Millie up to? I will see you first week of March. Charles misses his Gran, and merry Christmas from Walt and me,

Fi

p.s. How is Harry Landy doing?

Merry Christmas. I'm alone this year. Bruce and Fiona are in Belgium, which is good. You know, that's good for them to be there.

The last time I wrote to you (in October) I was telling you about what had happened with Harry Landy, and the fact of the matter is that the events of October 22 are stuck right here at the front of my mind. I find myself thinking of Harry regularly, even more than I did before. Honestly, I get to imagining him living here. As horrible as it was that day, him walking from Washington to Arnold, and James and Marly half dead with terror, and all the things that could have happened but, mercifully, did not, I will admit, it felt wonderful the moment he showed up on <u>my</u> doorstep. And the whole time he was here—just the one night— I was, well, I suppose I just loved that he was here (even though I know the situation was awful awful). Does it make sense what I'm saying?

I went for a walk this morning before the rain started. When I woke up I knew it was going to rain because the scent of it was so strong, so I went on out in my boots. It wasn't too cold. The sky was dark gray and moving quickly. I walked on down toward the river along the path. Have I ever described the path to you? I don't know that I've ever written it down at all. I love to go down the path by myself.

You cross the street from my driveway and there is a magnolia as tall as two light poles, and beside it is a little opening you might not notice if you were passing by, but there it is. You tuck in and then you're in the trees. In winter it's rather easier, whereas in the thick of summer it's much more like walking into a tunnel made by dryads, but anyway you walk in and then the path becomes clear after a few feet. There are others on the street who use the path, and sometimes the boys from the neighborhood behind will come through with their fishing poles and tackle boxes and use the path. I love to see that. It reminds me of the past when everything was right, you know that way boys walk, heads down, strong backs, kicking at the ground. But you walk through and the trees are all skinny and tall and there is one massive old oak, which fell, oh, maybe fifteen years ago now during a big storm, and it's just there along the path and you have to go around it or over it, and I go around it now. It's covered with a thick, bright green moss and lichen the color of those light mint Tic Tacs and usually you see some little thing or another scurrying around, like chipmunks or birds. Once there was a robin who had her nest there in the corner of a branch. She had her nest there for a few years, but then one morning it was gone, probably a fox. Anyway, I like to pass the fallen oak and see all the things to which it generously plays the host, letting all sorts feast. That old tree just makes me feel good. A bit past the tree there's a steep climb down to the water level, but there are some roots and stones that give me purchase, and I take a walking stick typically. I forgot to mention that, my walking stick. I found it some years ago now, there off the path. There is moss rather all the way down along the edges, and it's just this beautiful green, and then you're down at the edge of the river, and there is the gray moving water. I love to see it. The river, and the journey down, and then I walk along for a while, usually. I'll fish trash out from the edges sometimes and tuck it in my pocket. Sometimes I see herons. It smelled cold this morning, and rainy, and there's of course the briny must of the water, that smell, and the rotting trunks and leaves from the fall, and I love all of this, but it's melancholy, too, in a way. It's hard to explain it exactly, but it is gorgeous and melancholy all at once. I won't be able to see it, at some point, and when I can't see it I won't be able to go down there alone, which is really the only way I like to go down at all. A companion would spoil it, I think, though of course you'd be welcome to come along. I like to go down to get away from everything man-made and I feel like I'm far out in the wild, and then I find I can think. Anyway, by the time I got back up to the house I was ready for a cup of tea and writing some letters, and later I'll make a cherry pie and take it over for dinner with Trudy and Millie. Millie's husband is dead, and Trudy's been divorced longer than me. We'll play cards and listen to Christmas records. Millie has an ancient record player.

TO: customerservice@kindredproject.org
FROM: sybilvanantwerp@aol.com
DATE: Dec 28, 2014 07:54 PM
SUBJECT: HERE GOES NOTHING (Attn: Basam)

Hello Basam,

I hope you still work here because I have decided to send in my spit to see what kind of mutt I am. Please do be sure, once you run it through your machines and get whatever you need, that it's thrown in the bin. I hate the thought they would take the DNA of an old woman like myself and God forbid try to clone me. I wonder, are you a reader? I could never trust a person who wasn't a reader, though my doctor says I am going to go blind here in the not too distant future, at which point I suppose I will become a nonreader. Did you read the book *Never Let Me Go* by Kazuo Ishiguro? I am haunted by it. How long should I expect to wait before I am contacted with my results? Additionally, it's terribly unfortunate about your home in Syria. And of course I apologize for the offense I caused when our correspondence began, flippantly referring to your foreignness as being "Indian." I was worked up and I often find myself behaving with less civility over e-mail, and now as I type this I do feel rather ashamed of that carelessness. I hope you will forgive me. How old are your children? I had three children, but I've two now, one of whom seems determined to make a life as far from me as possible. Anyway, they will be the reason for which I'm embarking on this ridiculous venture of DNA testing. Did I mention to you I'm adopted? Parentage of unknown origin, and now the family decides it wants to know. Even my grandchildren are heckling me. From which institution did you receive your engineering degree?

Kind regards,
Sybil Van Antwerp

TO: sybilvanantwerp@aol.com
FROM: customerservice@kindredproject.org
DATE: Dec 29, 2014 01:19 PM
SUBJECT: Re: HERE GOES NOTHING (Attn: Basam)

Dear Ms. Van Antwerp,

I do continue to work for Kindred Project, but please allow me to clarify that I work in an office with a team of customer service representatives from the company and your DNA is not en route to my office specifically. We do not conduct DNA testing here; it is outsourced to labs around the country, so I will not personally receive, process, or dispose of your sample, but I can assure you it will be handled with professionalism and care. It will be six to eight weeks before you will hear about your results.

Your apology is noted, and previous offenses are forgiven. You are not the first person to mis-assign my ethnicity, and you will unfortunately not be the last.

I am a reader, but I have not read the book you mentioned. I will add it to my list and see if it is available at the library near my home. My children are ten and thirteen, a boy and a girl. I am sorry about your oncoming blindness, and moreover, sorry for the loss of your other child. While I have mercifully not lost a child, I have lost many family members, my home, my country, my religion, so I think I can understand a little of your grief, though when my brother died in the war it toppled my mother, so perhaps that specific grief, that of a mother losing her son, I cannot. My degree is from a university in Egypt called Kafr El Sheikh.

Please don't hesitate to reach out with additional questions! Thank you for contacting Kindredproject.org.

Basam

Sybil Van Antwerp
17 Farney Rd.
Arnold, MD 21012

Sybil,

I was clearing out some things and I found boxes of our letters. I went back to see if I could find the oldest ones and look at me! I'd forgotten the circumstances of the first letter you wrote me. I think we started more regular letters when I moved to CT in high school, the first was when you wrote to me from Camp Cedar Ridge when you went for the month the summer after jr. high—when your mother first had cancer. I cannot believe I've got it. I was so jealous of you that summer off to sleepaway camp while I was babysitting my cousins! I reread a bunch of the letters, and with mixed feelings. On one hand, it took me back to that time, and it was a dear feeling. Not nostalgia, exactly, but something like comfort—maybe some sympathy for who we were then. On the other hand, seeing things now as an adult through the lens of who we were as children is—there is something painful or uncomfortable about it, and now, knowing how things would go with Margaret's sickness. I had forgotten about Felix not speaking after your mother died. Didn't that go on for a couple of years? I can't believe I'd forgotten that. I've enclosed a few. I am happy to send more. I hope it isn't too hard reading them.

I'm reading Travels with Charley by John Steinbeck (which is charming—an intellectual cross-country road trip). What are you reading?

Love,

Rosalie

Rosalie Boyd
679 Holtermann Street
Philadelphia, Pa.

August 1, 1953

Dear Rosalie,

I'm having a fine time at camp even though the cabin where we sleep is filthy and sweltering. I sleep on the bottom bunk and the girl who sleeps above me, Thelma Mariani, shifts endlessly during the night, so I'm always waking up from the shaking and creaking. Some of the girls are OK, but usually I do things by myself or with one of the counselors Danielle, who is a college senior at Smith. I like the weaving and the canoeing. There are some forced group activities, like we played capture the flag a few nights ago, and there was a mystery scavenger hunt thing you had to do with your cabin, and those are the things I'd rather not do, but you are forced to participate. I brought the Space Trilogy (C. S. Lewis) and a bunch of Isaac Asimovs, but I'll finish those soon. It's stupid I'm here. If I was at home I could be helping with Felix. I got a letter from my dad yesterday. My mom's first treatment just finished and he said her hair is falling out and she can't really get out of bed because she feels so sick and throws up multiple times a day. I think he told me so when I get home I won't be surprised. Have you seen her? I can't even picture what she will look like without hair. I dreamed about it, but actually in the dream it was supposed to be her (without her hair) but in my dream it was a bald Doris Day. So that was weird. I'm really worrying about Felix. I miss him. I miss you, too, but I'll be home on Aug. 22.

Xoxo,

Sybil

Rosalie Boyd
9 Dover Place
Hamden, Conn.

October 24, 1955

Dear Rosalie,

Thanks for your letter. I'm glad you like your new school, and it's a drag about your chemistry teacher. You would think they would have better things to do than to discover new ways to torment teenagers. How was the dance? Have you seen Lee since? Do you <u>like him</u> like him?

Things are OK here. Boring. I didn't go to our homecoming dance. Nobody asked me and it would have been embarrassing to show up alone. Even NANCY PRUITT had a date (a boy from Belvedere). I cut my hair short. I'm doing some filing in my dad's office. He's got a new secretary. See how boring everything is? I'm telling you about my dad's work staff.

OK, the most interesting thing going on for me is that I wrote a letter to C. S. Lewis and he wrote me back! I was writing asking about if he would write any new worlds, and he said that he couldn't be sure about that, but that he was always thinking up new things. He told me there will be more books in The Chronicles of Narnia series, and he gave me a couple of hints about what happens! He suggested I read the series <u>The Lord of the Rings</u>, which came out last year and is written by a friend of his, so I bought the first book and I started it last night. It's excellent so far, much denser than Mr. Lewis's stories. His letter to me was wonderful. He's very kind, and you can sort of hear his voice from his novels in his letter-writing voice. I am working on a letter back to him.

What are you reading? Miss you. Write me,

Sybil

Rosalie Boyd
9 Dover Place
Hamden, Conn.

March 1, 1958

Dear Rosalie,

Mom died yesterday. I went home Monday because my dad called up to tell me she was declining suddenly and it was probably time, so I got the bus. It was while she was sleeping. I'm not sure when I'll go back to school. I might forgo the term. I don't feel like I can leave Felix. He's not speaking, not a single word since she died, and he won't leave my sight. He'd started sleeping in my bed when I went to school, and I can't coax him out.

The funeral is going to be on Sunday at the church. I hope you can come. I miss you so, so much.

Love,

Sybil

Mrs. Sybil vanAntwerp
17 Farney Rd.
Arnold, MD 21012

January 31, 2015

Dear Mrs. vanAntwerp,

My name is Caroline Dobsen and I am a junior at Broadneck High School. I am taking AP Government this year and we have an assignment to interview someone who worked in the judicial system at a federal or state level and write a 7-8 page paper due at the end of the semester. My grandfather told me about you because he thought you lived close to me. I live in Arundel on the Bay. My grandfather was a lawyer and he said he knew you from some cases he tried in the 1970s and 80s. I looked you up in the white pages online. It said your number was unlisted but had your address. I don't live very far away from you, so I wanted to ask if you would let me interview you and write my paper about you. I've actually thought I might want to go to law school.

My phone number is 515-5988 and my email address is carocarodobby@gmail.com, if you want to do that.

I get out of school at 3:15 but I have basketball practice until five. I could meet after that or on a weekend. It probably wouldn't take that long. Thank you.

Sincerely,

Caroline Dobsen

February 16, 2015

VAN ANTWE, SYBIL
17 FARNEY RD
ARNOLD MD 21012-1358
USA

Dear SYBIL VAN ANTWE:

Enclosed you will find the results of your DNA testing processed by LabCorp, as part of your membership with Kindredproject.org. These findings will give you an idea of your genetic makeup according to nations, as found against our entire body of DNA, although your results are independent and have not been linked to the results of any other individual.

Please do not hesitate to send any questions you may have to the Customer Service Team of KINDRED PROJECT (customer service@kindredproject.org).

Felix Stone
7 Rue de la Papillon
84220 Gordes
FRANCE

February 18, 2015

Dear Felix,

How are you and how is Stewart? How is he recovering from the surgery on his shoulder? Shoulder surgeries are terrible with recovery I've heard. It's really too bad. He is very good at tennis.

I am writing for one reason only and that is to tell you I got my DNA test results back from the lab. Apparently I am fully one-half British (I suppose this includes Scotland and Wales, wouldn't it? Northern Ireland?), a quarter Native American, which surprised me but explains my dark eyes and hair, and a quarter bits of this and that, Russia and Iberia. Doesn't it seem unlikely, though? Couldn't they just slap down anything and send it off? And anyway, even if it's true, what's interesting about it? Aren't we all just ready mixes of everything now that the world is so small and everyone going this way and that—but it's neither here nor there, Felix, I logged into my profile on the website and it's got my little colored world map and a corresponding pie chart simple enough for a second grader to decipher. It does make one think, but it's not that interesting. I called the children to tell them, and they were happy to know. Fiona asked if I was glad to have done it and I told her it doesn't really much make a difference to me. So that's that. A little British, a little Native American, a little Russian. Classic American mutt!

You know when you fiddle around in the webpage, now that I've sent the spit and they have my DNA, there are all these other features. I asked my friend Basam (he's a Syrian refugee engineer customer service representative) a little more about the box you can check to link to others. I'm not going to do that, of course, seems like the most foolish thing in the world, doesn't it? And like I said, how do I know it's not a scam and they tell you this person is related to you, but they're not? The whole system could be—very well it's likely it is—run on the unrealistic hopes of gullible schmucks desperate for family. Thank you, no. How would one know if such a claim could be believed, and anyway, it's irrelevant. I can admit that it's been a little bit interesting, but I'll not carry it further.

Changing topic, I didn't tell you a few weeks ago I met with a high school student for an interview. She's writing a paper about me because of the clerkship. When she came to the house in sweatpants about five sizes too large and her wet hair thrown up in a mess on top of her head I thought, well, she looks about as bright as a root cellar, but she asked me good questions, as a matter of fact. The child knew something about government and politics. I did enjoy thinking about everything again. She recorded the conversation as if she was Bob Woodward. She took it seriously, and I appreciated that. Somehow we got onto the topic of letter writing. I think I mentioned to her that being a clerk requires sharp writing skills, and then it was her wanting to know how I learned to write well, so I told her it's just practice, like everything. She wanted to know with whom I exchange correspondence, and I told her: anyone! Of course the letters I cherish most would be of little or no interest to her, but I showed her a few of the more remarkable letters—the one from Jackie Kennedy, the one from Walt Disney. She was <u>astounded</u> that people write back, and of course I told her: people are just people. Famous or not. Silly, but then it was fun going back in. I sat for the rest of the afternoon once she'd gone thumbing through some of the correspondence I've saved. There are hundreds of letters, into the thousands I expect, and to think, each one has a counterpart somewhere, even if it's in a trash heap.

Please send me your schedule for June as soon as you have it. I don't expect you to sit around my house for the whole month, but it would be nice to be able to make some sort of plan. There will be a parade of homes downtown the second weekend, and I can take a look at the chamber of commerce website to see if there is anything else worth doing. There are plenty of outdoor festivities on Friday and Saturday nights in the summer and of course the birds are asquawk at your coming. Remind me, do you land in Washington or Baltimore on the first? I am going out with Mick Watts again. Not a word. Not one single word.

Love,

Syb

TO: customerservice@kindredproject.org
FROM: sybilvanantwerp@aol.com
DATE: Mar 6, 2015 11:32 PM
SUBJECT: HELLO (Attn: Basam)

Hi Basam, How is your wife doing with her English course? Did she quit at the restaurant? What that boss is doing to her is harassment, and surely she can find restaurant work anywhere. And how are the children? Did Zoha get glasses? Surely that's all it is.

My son Bruce has a friend who works in city planning in Northern Virginia at a firm with branches across the US. He said he would be willing to take a look at your resume. His work is like the work you trained in, transportation infrastructure. This man, his name is Dale Woodson, is honestly rather dull, and the poor man has a stutter he goes to unsuccessful pains to conceal, but he has been a friend of Bruce's (that is Bruce, my son, who is a lawyer and is also honestly a bit dull, but he is also reliable and kind and takes care of me) since grade school and I've known him a long time. He is practical and he's made a good life for himself. I explained your situation, but I DID NOT EXPLAIN HOW WE HAVE COME TO BE FRIENDS, SO PLEASE DO NOT MENTION THE DNA TESTING AS IF I AM A SUBJECT OF SCIENTIFIC RESEARCH.

The best course is for you to send me your resume, I'll look it over and clean it up for you, as we have previously discussed, and then I will send the resume back to you and you can contact Dale directly, referencing Bruce.

Regarding the DNA: What, precisely, happens when one checks the box? I suppose once I do, it's done. Not something I could really take back.

With warm regards,
Sybil Van Antwerp

Sybil Van Antwerp
17 Farney Road
Arnold, MD
21012 USA

30 May 2015

Dear Sybil,

Yesterday was your birthday. When I imagine you it is still in the house we shared, though I know you have not lived there now for almost thirty years. Because I cannot envision any other place I think often of it, and our life there feels like only a short time ago. Sometimes, like a test, I wander that house in my mind and see if I can still open every door and see what was inside. I make sure I can account for the entire house, down to the details like what photos we had on the mantel. How the cupboards were organized—cereal beside the refrigerator. Mugs and bowls over the stove. I step the stones from the back door off the kitchen to the garden.

The children told me you know of my cancer from Rosalie. I'm glad she was the one to tell you. Rosalie always seemed more like a sister to you than a friend and I have been grateful for that. We were fortunate to have Rosalie and Lars as family and friends. It's rare, I think. The children have been back and forth to Belgium over the past few months, as I assume you know. The fact is, I won't live very much longer. They have tried all sorts of things and they don't say it isn't working, but I can feel the cancer. Bruce wishes I would fly back and go to the Mayo Clinic. I have no desire to return to America. I want to be here at home for as many days as I can.

They call it "fighting." Fighting cancer. Fighting through treatment. Putting up a fight. But you know I am not a fighting man. I am far more inclined to surrender. I'm ready to go, but I keep this to myself. Sometimes I imagine you being here. I think you would let me go. Lina holds on. She takes me to the grave-yard to see the gravestones of my parents and it brings me a great deal of comfort. I remember visiting the site as a younger man and that sense of grief, like my chest filling with wet sand. But now I feel only peace there knowing I will see my mother and father and Gilbert again. Lina is not doing very well. It seems as though she has become sick with something else, thin, sad, while I have become sick with my cancer. Felix visited me. Did you know that? He came on the train. It was lovely to see him again. You know how he is. He made me laugh and that was the great-est gift of all. I do regret I won't see my brother again. The last time was when we met in London. It was years ago now. I can't recall.

You are a remarkable woman. Solid as a mountain. Intelli-gent. I loved your intelligence first, that smart brightness in your eyes, the look you had when I met you—like you were ready, whatever was coming, you were ready. With you I felt formida-ble. You say what you mean. You are well able for the hard things, much more than I am. Your career was astounding. It makes me proud. You still occupy a large space in me. I felt honored those years we were together that you entrusted me with your stones, and I still keep them. I want you to know that, even though it's not what I'm writing for. I want you to know I keep your stones as safe as ever. But here is what I'm trying to say, I am trying to get around to something, I'm not sure precisely what.

Gilbert's dying. It became the whole thing. You, Bruce and Fiona, my brother, our friends, my work, the house, our life, all of that was sitting on the sidelines, but I was in the ring wrestling, bloody, half-dead, with Gill's death. Parenting the other two, try-ing to help them with their own grief, was like acting. I could say what needed to be said, but I was only thinking of myself in the ring with Gill's death. I have asked Bruce and Fiona about that period of time. I was surprised to learn they're both in therapy. I think neither of us was able to shepherd them in those first crucial months, submerged, completely, in the swamp water of despair. We were needing the same thing, you and I, a temple in which to tuck away and disappear from the earth, to mourn at the altar of our desolation, but we had the children, so we could not. Could we have held onto each other? I've wondered. We did the best we could and it was not enough. The four of us came away injured, but is there any other way for a person to come through? Oh, Gilbert. I do hope there is a heaven as I have always believed. I hope I will see him and know him there. I believe I've been looking forward to death on one hand.

Here I am finally making my way, though slowly. It was this reason I had to leave. I was not up to the task of grieving Gilbert's death and still being a decent father or a decent husband. I know that by the time we separated it was what we both wanted. Things had become so wretched, but this was my failure. I regret it even now. It's one of the things I regret. I am grateful to have fallen in love with Lina, something that was only possible because Lina was so distant from all that I'd left when I left you. But what I want to say to you is this: I cannot take back things I said to you in those early dark days. Oh, that we could have the wisdom of age earlier! What happened to Gill could have happened to any child. I blamed you, but you were not at fault. Terrible accidents happen all the time to many, many people. The grief that must fill the world is incomprehensible. Our small dose felt as large as the sun, didn't it? And it persists. I'll never forget the day he died, the way you knelt on the floor and wept, and I left you there, unable to touch you, blaming you when there was nothing to blame. Sybil, forgive me!

Now that I'm dying it seems much simpler than it ever did before. Living, I mean. There is no parallel universe. There is no "what could have been if only." In some ways this has brought me a great deal of peace. In other ways it is bitter. How cruel life is only this long. Now that I see clearly, I'd like more time. It's not to be. I can't exactly explain it, but I feel the dying. Did you read that remarkable book about cancer? <u>The Emperor of All Maladies</u>. The emperor, indeed. Mukherjee. Remarkable. I think of it often. It's taken me an entire afternoon with a nap after the third paragraph to finish this letter.

I'm ready to go, but I don't think Fiona is OK. Please make sure she is OK. Dear Sybil, I do love you. The children are fortunate it's not you they're losing. You've been a wonderful mother to them. The first thing I will do is kiss Gilbert for you.

I'd like to hear from you. Not a demand, merely a hope, but either way, until we meet again, and I believe we will—we must—with love,

Daan

(cont. June 6, 2015, previous pages UNSENT)

AMERICAN PHARAOH WINS THE TRIPLE CROWN!

A descendant (some great-great-great-grandson) of Secretariat. Isn't that just wonderful? Oh, it's just absolutely a smash. I'm delighted, and thinking of you, of course. Of course.

TO: sybilvanantwerp@aol.com
FROM: dna@kindredproject.org
DATE: Jun 17, 2015 11:52 PM
SUBJECT: MEET YOUR KINDRED. Congratulations! You have a DNA match.

Dear Kindred member,

You have a DNA match. To access the details of this information, please log into your Kindred profile by clicking here.

Our best,
The team at Kindred Project

Ms.Van Antwerp
17 Farney Rd.
Arnold, MD 21012

June 28, 2015

Dear Ms. Van Antwerp,

Thank you for taking the time to talk to me about your career as the chief clerk for Judge Donnelly in the Circuit Court. Your career was pretty cool. I got my final grade for the quarter and the paper was 50% of the grade. I got an A! My teacher didn't know you lived around the corner from the school, and she wants you to come speak to her class next year. (I'm sorry, I told her you hate public speaking.) I wanted you to know how much I liked interviewing you, and even enjoyed writing the paper. (It ended up being eleven pages! I copied it for you . . . I hope you like it and hopefully I didn't get anything wrong.) My dad's mom died when I was four and my mom's mom died about two years ago with Alzheimer's disease, but you reminded me a little bit of her. Actually your juice glasses are the same ones she had. My mom said they were very cool in the 70s/80s. Now that kind of stuff is vintage, and cool again.

I loved seeing all your letters. How many letters do you think you've written during your life? When did you start? How do you decide who to write to? I don't think I have ever received a real letter. I wouldn't even know how to write a good one. How do you start and what do you say? I wanted to ask you if you have time, maybe you would write me a letter? Totally OK if you're too busy, but I promise if you write to me I will write you back.

Sincerely,

Caroline Dobsen

TO: customerservice@kindredproject.org
FROM: sybilvanantwerp@aol.com
DATE: Jun 30, 2015 07:04 AM
SUBJECT: HELLO (Attn: Basam)

Basam,

Are you there?? JUST SEEING THIS. How is it that I have a DNA match? I have not checked the box!!!!!!!!!!!

TO: sybilvanantwerp@aol.com
FROM: customerservice@kindredproject.org
DATE: Jun 30, 2015 02:34 PM
SUBJECT: Re: HELLO (Attn: Basam)

Dear Ms. Van Antwerp,

I hope you are well. I have just now logged into your profile, and it appears that the box was checked. Do you have any memory of doing such a thing? Did you give account access to someone else, like your brother? The date of this change was June 15.

Please don't hesitate to reach out with additional questions! Thank you for contacting Kindredproject.org.

Basam

TO: customerservice@kindredproject.org
FROM: sybilvanantwerp@aol.com
DATE: Jun 30, 2015 06:01 PM
SUBJECT: RE: Re: HELLO (Attn: Basam)

NO

TO: customerservice@kindredproject.org
FROM: sybilvanantwerp@aol.com
DATE: Jul 1, 2015 06:43 AM
SUBJECT: RE: RE: Re: HELLO (Attn: Basam)

Hell. I think I know what must have happened. You see, my brother had been visiting from France and I'd let everything pile up, not touched the computer. He left June 15 and I discovered a letter in the stack of post to which I'd yet to attend from my ex-husband. We haven't spoken in years, but he's dying. The letter was very troubling. I opened a bottle of rum (this is something I rarely do). I got on the computer and I was tooling around. I must have clicked the box. What can be done? No interest in this DNA MATCH. CAN YOU DELETE IT? PLEASE HELP. SYBIL

TO: sybilvanantwerp@aol.com
FROM: customerservice@kindredproject.org
DATE: Jul 1, 2015 11:03 AM
SUBJECT: RE: RE: RE: Re: HELLO (Attn: Basam)

Dear Ms. Van Antwerp,

I'm afraid we cannot delete the match because, well, I guess it's difficult to know exactly how to say this, but if you have a person with a DNA match, that match exists outside of our system. I hope this is coming across correctly. The person with whom you share DNA is, in fact, alive in the world. Furthermore, at the time you were sent notification of the match, this member would have also received a similar communication. I can ask my manager about the possibility of blocking contact between this individual and yourself. Would you like me to do that?

Please don't hesitate to reach out with additional questions! Thank you for contacting Kindredproject.org.

Basam

TO: customerservice@kindredproject.org
FROM: sybilvanantwerp@aol.com
DATE: Jul 5, 2015 02:41 PM
SUBJECT: RE: RE: RE: RE: Re: HELLO (Attn: Basam)

Would blocking communications be reversible?

Caroline Dobsen
7864 Windmere Rd.
Annapolis, MD 21403

July 15, 2015

Dear Caroline,

I am pleased to hear your paper turned out a good score. It was well written, if a little exaggerated. There were a few dates you mixed up, but that's no matter to anyone but myself, and the undergraduate college I attended was Bryn Mawr in Pennsylvania, but otherwise I did think it well done. Concise, efficient with language, good spelling, intriguing structure. I will say, I noticed that you rather painted me in a heroic light. It's kind of you, but I was no hero, Caroline. I made errors, decisions that bore lasting effects on the lives of strangers. It doesn't matter that it's not in your paper, it doesn't matter at all, but it matters to me that you know that.

I hope you are having an enjoyable summer. I believe you mentioned lifeguarding as a summer position. You must be QUITE a swimmer to put yourself in charge of the lives of children. At which of the community pools do you sit on the stand? Will you take any trips? It escapes me if you have siblings.

I'm sorry you lost your grandmother to Alzheimer's. My brother-in-law is dealing with the same thing and it's ugly ugly. Awful to witness, and probably worse if you're inside the body, but nobody knows and that makes it worse. I feel sorry any child has to bear witness to a thing like that.

Those juice glasses with the stripe and circle did have a moment. I've had them for such a long time it's amazing the color doesn't wear off, but of course I don't stick them in the dishwasher. Hand wash only with a soft cloth.

Getting to your questions about the letter writing. I'll start by saying your note heartened me because here is a secret: my letters have been far more meaningful to me than anything I did with the law. The letters are the mainstay of my life, where I was only practicing law for thirty years or so. The clerkship was my job; the letters amount to who I am. I haven't the foggiest idea how many I've written. I certainly didn't keep track along the way, and I've never gone back to count the ones I've received. More than a thousand, I guess. I have written letters since I was a child. I wrote to the odd author or teacher, cousins I rarely saw. I wrote to the local fire chief, Harry Truman, people like that. I had a pen pal, she was a friend who lived down the street from me and then she moved away in high school, and we are still pen pals writing every month or six weeks, give or take, for sixty years. We married brothers (I divorced mine). Oh! Hers is the one with Alzheimer's. That's where it started, I guess, though I hadn't ever thought of it like that until now. Rosalie Boyd. (Well, now she's Van Antwerp, too.) She is my daughter's godmother. How's all that for a big complicated mess?

I write to anyone that strikes me. Friends, lawmakers, editors, teachers, diplomats, authors. Authors are my favorite. It's harder now, of course, because with the internet people are e-mailing (it's faster, simpler, less fussy than having to have the materials, the pen, the moment at the desk, the stamp, etc.) and it can be more difficult to find an address, but usually if you really try, you will. And one ought to try. An e-mail can in no way replace a written letter. It does concern me that one day all the advancement of technology will do away with the post, but I hope to be dead and gone long before then.

To your question of 'how': I sit down at my desk with a stack of the letter writing paper and the pens I like. My desk faces a small window toward the river and there are honeysuckle bushes beneath it, which, in summer, attract hummingbirds, and my garden lies beyond. The house will be silent, or if I am feeling passionate, Tchaikovsky or Stravinsky from the CD player. I'll have a glass of water or a cup of tea. Typically I write on Mondays, Wednesdays, and Fridays for about two hours. Whatever I don't finish gets pushed to Saturday, and of course, if the mood strikes me at off times (a shocking current event or anger, usually), I'll sit down then as well. I mail-order my letter writing paper from England; once I discovered it, I quit trying anything else. I visit the post office once a month for stamps. I never buy seasonal stamps, only your classic stars and stripes, because there is a certain structure, an ORDER, that needs to be obeyed. If you keep the mechanism in order, then the contents of the correspondence, the material of the letters I mean, can go anywhere. Be anything. You can write to anyone. You can say anything you like.

I write slowly. A letter might take me an hour or more. I do not rush. I think through each sentence. My hand does not get tired. You mustn't rush. When you rush you pen things you didn't mean and you tire. It takes patience to say exactly what one means, to think of the right word. Sometimes I write a draft and mark it up, then write a clean copy to send. I believe one ought to be precious with communication. Remember: words, especially those written, are immortal. Sometimes, Caroline, the easiest inroad is to begin with a thank you, for a gift or a kindness or a letter, you know, and then take it from there. Answer every question they've asked, and ask your own, and you will have created a never-ending circuit of curiosity and learning.

You're most welcome to write me back if you'd like, but my suggestion would be to think of someone who is far away, someone you don't see frequently or speak to often on the phone but dearly wish you could, and write to them instead. I wish you the very best.

Warm regards,

Sybil Van Antwerp

The College of English
University of Maryland, College Park
College Park, MD 20742

TO: Melissa Genet, Dean of the College of English
FROM: Sybil Van Antwerp

August 5, 2015

I am writing for the fifth and final time to you before I am forced to escalate my request that you reconsider your position on auditing courses in the College of English. Two years have passed since your first refusal, two years of my life I cannot repeat, and I would like to think you were simply taking a bit of time to get your wits about you in the position of dean. A modern literature course would be preferable—1800s at the earliest. Patience waning.

(cont. Sept. 12, 2015, previous pages UNSENT)

Daan died last night. I wanted to tell you that.

Rosalie Van Antwerp
33 Orange Lane
Goshen, CT 06756

September 12, 2015

Dear Rosalie,

I didn't tell you Daan wrote, it was back in May, a rather long letter saying a great deal. I read it again and again. It is a terrible and wonderful letter. Daan never wrote to anyone, but reading it I wonder why. Several times I sat down to write him back, but my mind was blank, an event that I cannot recall at any previous time. Fiona called this morning to say he's dead. She was at his side. I never did send him a letter. The paper with his name at the top and some inadequate babble is started right here on my desk. I'm looking at it. Oh, Rosalie. My life has felt enormous, but what do I have to show for it?

This morning I walked down to the river and I was thinking about our trip to Lake Saint-Pierre. I did this on purpose, as punishment, perhaps, self-flagellation, and now I'm making myself write to you about it. I rarely let my mind go there, Rosalie. If there is a map of the world in my mind, I don't look there at the border of Canada and the US, but this morning I tried to remember. I even went looking for photographs of the trip, but I guess I've thrown them all away, but what I was trying to remember was how we were before Gilbert died, what was the last way we were—my whole family. That morning. That week. What was my family like? Daan had been talking to someone at Boston College about teaching. I'd forgotten about that, but it came back to me. It was a position in the school of languages. In the weeks leading up to the trip there had been heavy tension between us because he wanted to take the position, and of course I was totally unwilling to consider leaving my job, but I do think we'd largely managed to leave that impasse at home and I remember laughing a great deal on this trip. Do you remember? You were very pregnant and wearing those awful drapey dresses without shape and your ankles were terribly swollen, and I remember being up on the patio with a bottle of whiskey one evening and laughing until we cried over your ankles. That must mean things were good if I can remember all that laughing. And the children were at such wonderful ages then. I made myself think about the day he died. I went back to the day and put my outfit back together (I could get that far, denim pants, white top) but when I tried to follow myself back down on the dock where I was when he dove into the water, I couldn't. It is as if, in my mind, there is a sentry standing outside the locked room of this memory—it won't let me in. It's my memory! He won't allow it, stands unyielding. It is like blindness. So that's as far as I got. I couldn't get in. But I know what happened. He dove into the lake, he hit the rock shelf and snapped his neck. I have this image in my mind of his back, slick, he's lying on his side. It's his body. Beads of water on his tan back. They must have pulled him out—who? Did I? And laid him on his side on the dock. There were two moles on his back and I must have stared at them because I see his tan, wet back, the two moles. Did I scream for help? Who got him out of the lake? Was it me? In my memory, it's all silence. It has been a long time since I returned to that. It's been years. It's possible it's been decades. What do you remember? Suddenly I am hungry for these memories. Write me and tell me what you remember.

Daan's funeral will be in three weeks, the first Saturday of October, but I can't possibly attend. Bruce said he would fly with me. He and the children and Marie will of course attend. I've just been on the phone to Felix, who thinks I should go. He says you always always go to the funeral, and, of course, in principle, I agree. Perhaps I will go. I did always want to see where he was from.

Syb

Postscript: I've been reading <u>Rebecca</u> by Daphne du Maurier, but it's taking me ages. What are you reading?

Kindredproject.org MESSAGING PORTAL

TO: Henrietta Gleason
FROM: Sybil Van Antwerp
DATE: September 21, 2015

Good morning,

A little over two months ago I received notification from this website
of a DNA match. This was a mistake. I had no intention of opening
my information to connection with other Kindred users. As it turns
out I did check the box by mistake when I was drunk. I'm also going
blind. (I am not an alcoholic; I rarely drink. It was a bad set of circumstances.) I was planning to ignore the information, but a few
days ago I opened the notification. It appears that you and I are a
DNA match.
My name is Sybil Stone Van Antwerp. I live in Annapolis, Maryland
(the capital of the state of Maryland), and I grew up more or less in
Philadelphia. I have two grown children and three grandchildren. I
was adopted from within the US.
Perhaps this DNA matching business is nothing. I have spent most
of the last year assuming it was all a scam, honestly, but here I am
coming to you nonetheless. I think I would like to hear from you so I
can at last shut off this particular valve in my mind.

Warm regards,
Sybil Van Antwerp

<ERROR> <User VAN ANTWERP, SYBIL>
Re: Message to Henrietta Gleason
FROM: KINDRED PROJECT Account Services
DATE: SEPTEMBER 21, 2015

The user you are trying to contact has an account that has been either temporarily suspended or deactivated. Your message will be delivered if/when the user reactivates the account.
Please contact accounts@kindredproject.org for further information.

TO: customerservice@kindredproject.org
FROM: sybilvanantwerp@aol.com
DATE: Sep 25, 2015 10:00 AM
SUBJECT: NEEDING YOUR HELP (Attn: Basam)

Good morning, Basam. Have you got your resume together yet? I've told you previously I'll be glad to clean it up for you. Just send the bones. Certainly a job change would be much better for your family. Certainly the pay would be much higher than whatever you make at Kindred, and your wife could quit working altogether if it's what she wants, though you haven't said as much.

Can you look in my profile and see where I sent a message to Henrietta Gleason, the woman to whom it appears I match a significant measure of DNA? There is an error. Do you think you could log into her profile the way you frequently log into mine and find her e-mail address for me? Or a phone number or an address? Now that I've decided to get in touch I am unable to reach her. (And do you know, I'm not even sure I want to be in touch, but I like to have options.)

My husband's died as of a few weeks ago. Well, he was my ex-husband. I'm booked to attend his funeral, which is in Belgium, in about ten days. I dread it, but you know, I get to feeling sorry for myself, and then I think of you and remember it could be worse. Anyway, I tell you so you know I'll be away from the computer for some time. Send your resume when it suits.

Warm regards, Sybil Van Antwerp

Daan has died, which I've already said. If I write it again and again, perhaps it will sink in. The funeral is in Belgium and I have my plane ticket. October 3 I leave. This will be my first time out of the country, aside from the one cursed trip to Canada, which I don't count.

I imagine myself at the church in the small town surrounded by people speaking a language I do not know and himself in the casket there with the lid folded open. It was a quarter century ago the last time I saw him. I think that's right, give or take. I can see him the day he left. I can see him walking into the tunnel at the airport beside Fiona. He had blond hair and he wore it rather long then. He had stayed very slim and I can see him walking down the tunnel beside Fiona wearing his denim and the leather loafers he loved. He was wearing a wool blazer and he had his traveling bag. I remember Fiona looked back at me over her shoulder. She gave me a little wave, nothing dramatic, she would be coming back in the summer. Here is a small detail I remember—I could see, as she turned her face back in the direction they were walking, that she was saying something to him, I could see her mouth moving, but of course they were too far away for me to know what she was saying. I hoped very much she was saying something about me, how I was standing there or some little thing, and I hoped, I really hoped, he said something back. I wanted him to look back the way Fiona had, but he didn't, and I guess probably up until that point it hadn't been true to me yet. I hadn't really believed it was happening, but then he was gone without looking back and a shock wave hit me deep down in my bone marrow. It felt like my body was vibrating, the way the air trembles after a gong is struck.

Why was I saying this?

Yes. I'm not sure if I can stomach that image I have of him

leaving that last day in all of his professorial stature being replaced by the shriveled, disease-ravaged corpse of an old man. I think that's the roundabout train of my thoughts. I'm terrified. However, one must attend the funeral. There is nothing I can think of more important than the prioritization of attendance to a funeral.

Someone is stalking me. After Judge Donnelly died, this individual contacted me with a letter, a rather crass and vengeful kind of letter, which was disturbing. I had not received anything of the sort in a long time, though it did remind me of when we were in the courthouse years, how Guy and I (and others) would receive those kinds of nasty missives from time to time, people disgruntled and hateful about the way a ruling had gone, and back then I did not have my address listed in the public record for that very reason. The subsequent note that arrived, though uncomfortable, did not make me afraid and I tried to put it out of my mind. However, after some time, I guess maybe another year went by and I received the third communication from this individual, but it was evident he or she had visited my house. I know it's true because in the letter, she or he (seems like a man) described my garden and my unique mailbox. You might wonder if I have any idea who this person is. I do not. They have signed their communications with two initials, and that is all. This individual threatened to pay additional visits to my house. I get the sense that the purpose of this is rather to make me feel afraid, and not likely to actually harm me in any way, and it's working. When I read it I felt frightened, really frightened, Colt. I can't think of the last time I had felt that way. I hate to feel afraid. I can think of nothing worse, so I imagine this person watching me as I go slowly blind. I imagine this, and when blind, how I won't even know, and I'm sure anyone would advise me to call the police, but I won't do that. What would they do other than send a patrol car over every so often? If I told Bruce and Fiona, they'd only fret or make me move (they're already trying to get me to go to an old people's home) and I have no interest in anything of that sort. I have considered alerting my neighbor, Theodore Lübeck. I did have a security system installed with a camera, but I'm confused about how it works, so I rarely turn it on.

Enough now. I'll let you know how things go regarding the funeral.

Ms. Joan Didion
30 E. 71st St. #5A
New York, NY 10021

October 6, 2015

Dear Joan,

It's the day of Daan's funeral (my ex-husband), and I've got the plane ticket sitting here on the desk on top of the book stack. At the last minute, three days ago, I didn't go to the airport. I simply didn't go. If I regret the decision, then so be it. My life is in winter anyway; only a little while left to nurse regrets. I went back and reread <u>The Year of Magical Thinking</u>. The first time I read it, years ago, I recall thinking I would return to it one day, and although my situation is different than yours, with all these years that separate Daan and me, I found so much of it put word to the way I do feel, whether I have any right to or not. Of course I really don't have the right.

Do let me know how you are getting on.

Sybil

TO: sybilvanantwerp@aol.com
FROM: Fiona.VanAntwerpBeau@cgemarchitects.com
DATE: Nov 1, 2015 06:15 AM
SUBJECT: Dad's funeral

Mom, I'm back in London now. Walt brought Charles back last week, but I stayed to help Lina go through some of Dad's things. The funeral was perfect. Held in the beautiful old Catholic church where Oma and Opa got married. I met some distant cousins, etc.

I'm having a hard time wrapping my mind around why you didn't come. Bruce said it's your fear of flying, fine. I know you don't travel and I've told myself that's why you haven't ever come to visit me in London, but with all your principles of propriety, all your tenets on how one ought to be . . . you attend a funeral! Even if it's someone you didn't know well, even if you had a grudge. Fine that he's not your husband anymore, but he was my father, Bruce's father, Gilbert's father. You should have been there. You know, a lot of times if I'm angry and I take a little time, my feelings will cool off, but the longer I sat with your not coming the angrier I got. Lina told me he wrote you a letter and waited for a reply, but you didn't write back. You, who sit holed up at home and writing letters to god knows who every day, and knowing full well he was dying. I don't understand you. I have never understood you.

Anyway, Dad left some things to you, a necklace of his mother's you must have said you liked, a book, I think. Maybe something else. Bruce has them. He said he'll see you in a couple weeks.

Fiona

Ms. Sybil S. Van Antwerp
17 Farney Rd.
Arnold, Maryland 21012
United State of America

9 November 2015

Dear Ms. Van Antwerp,

My name is Angela Bleeker, and I am an attorney with the law firm Drost & Drost in Brussels, Belgium. I want to start by extending my condolences for the loss of your ex-husband, Daan Van Antwerp. I have been in his employ for many years, as well as the employ of several members of his family. Daan was respectful and kind to me on the instances when we met to discuss the matter of his financials, and toward the end of his life, his estate.

You may or may not be surprised to learn that you are listed as an inheritor in Mr. Van Antwerp's last will and testament for a sizable sum of money from his holdings, which grew substantially about six years ago when his uncle passed away. I will need to speak with you over the phone in order to go over the specifics of what we will require in order to move these funds to the bank account of your choosing, but there was no phone number listed in any of the paperwork provided by your ex-husband. Enclosed with this letter is a form. Please fill it out at your earliest convenience with your most up-to-date contact information and fax it to the number provided at the top of the page. Alternatively, you can call the number provided at the bottom of this letter, email, or respond by mail.

I look forward to speaking with you at your earliest convenience.

Angela Bleeker, Lawyer

Drost & Drost Lawyers, Belgium

Ms. Van Antwerp
17 Farney Rd.
Arnold, MD
21012

December 18, 2015

Dear Ms. Van Antwerp,

Thank you for the puzzle book. I finished it in five days. I was surprised you continued writing to me on the fifteenth of the months when I haven't written you back in four months. Why did you keep writing? I was trying to tell you, without writing again, that I did not want to continue with the letters, but you didn't understand. This is my last letter to you.

Here is what has happened in the past five months:

1. I started tenth grade at my new school Maxwell Academy and they call it Second Year. The classes at the school are pretty good and the building is extremely nice. They assign much more homework. I have been put in the most advanced math classes, including a special course with only a few boys, and I'm the best in the class. They serve very good lunches, as good as what our cook makes (or better), and there is a water polo team, which I play on, and I'm better than 60% of the players. Patrick was my one friend there (I met him when I came at the end of First Year), but he moved to Delhi (INDIA) because his father took the ambassadorship assignment from President Obama.

2. There are several boys at my school who make fun of me for various reasons, including that my hair is greasy and I have extremely sweaty palms, sometimes so sweaty that they leave a handprint. (This started

over the summer. I saw a doctor and they tried putting shots of Botox in my hands, but it didn't help for more than 7 to 8 days.) They say I smell bad and they call me The Screamer because of the one freakout I had last year, which I told you about in my March 2015 letter. (Did you know I photocopy every letter before I send it so I can keep our letters in order and then they make sense and I can refer back to check things you or I have written in the past? They are kept in 2 three ring binders.) I hate when they call me Screamer. Any time they come near me I try to imagine I am climbing inside myself. It's hard to explain. The way I think of it is like I'm turning inside out sort of. I usually go quiet, but what's really crazy about it is that it feels like, inside, I actually am screaming.

3. I'm building a model Lusitania with a kit Susannah ordered for me from London.

4. I'm writing a new story.

5. My mom was in a mental hospital again, a different one, but she got out, and then she went to live with her parents in Santa Barbara. She left on October 6. I don't know if she will be coming back for Christmas. My sister Lauren is coming home, but not Susannah because she started new philanthropy in Peru. Lauren got engaged to Steve on Thanksgiving, but any time she talks to Dad about it she is crying, so I don't know if she's happy or sad. I definitely think it's sad, though I understand people cry with both sets of feelings. Her wedding will be on June 14, 2016.

6. Thor is awesome. Every day I take her for a long walk after school. She's super smart, so she doesn't have to be on a leash. Most recently I taught her the command "hide," so if I say it, she goes and hides behind a bush or

a car or something, and then when I say "come out" she jumps right back to me. It's amazing!

7. I'm reading the Foundation series by Isaac Asimov for the second time.

I think this will be my last letter. Don't forget the pact we made a long time ago when you promised you won't tell my dad anything I say in the letters unless I am in danger. I have always liked writing to you because it feels good. I have also liked that I would get a letter on the fifteenth of the month, which is nice and even to balance out the days, more or less, even though some months have more than 30 days and one month has less, but I don't want to do it anymore. Maybe you can write me one more time in order to finish this year, since I was the first one to ever write, but could you try to have the letter to me by December 31, 2015? That would really even things out well, although I've messed up the pattern the last few months. If you do write me again, I would like to know (a) how your vision is doing, (b) if the dean of the English school at University of Maryland let you into a class, (c) if you are still attending the garden club, and (d) if you went for dinner again with the dude from Texas.

Warm regards,

Harry Landy

TO: jameswlandy@gmail.com
FROM: sybilvanantwerp@aol.com
DATE: Dec 28, 2015 05:55 PM
SUBJECT: Harry

Hello James,

Well, typically I am keeping up with the goings-on of the Landys via Harry and his monthly updates, but the last few months he'd fallen off with them. I'd been expecting this for some time, as our habit of correspondence began when he was only in grade school, and now that he is in high school it becomes less and less likely he'll want to write letters to an old woman. I kept the letters going, but just as I was thinking it would be time to quit, earlier this week I did open a letter from Harry, and it quite surprised me for a number of reasons. James, has Marly gone and left you for good? I knew she was back in Sheppard Pratt last winter, but Harry indicated she went back again, and now she's gone to live with her mother and dad? James, your girls will be alright, but Harry is fragile. I have promised him I won't divulge the contents of his letters, but I am worried about the boy. I know you said it was necessary he change schools, but are you aware of what happens to the child at his new school? Do try and get it out of him, James.

Of course I write with warm regards, sending tidings of a Merry Christmas (belated) and a happy new year (early),

Sybil

Postscript: I am coming with Mick Watts to Washington—symphony and dinner.

Second postscript: I am watching this Donald Trump for the presidency in disbelief. The thing has legs, James. God save the queen. Now I've seen it all. I guess it's time to change my registration card and make my party allegiance official. You never thought you'd see that day, did you? Sybil Stone becomes a Democrat. That should be the title of my memoirs.

TO: customerservice@kindredproject.org
FROM: sybilvanantwerp@aol.com
DATE: Jan 6, 2016 10:05 AM
SUBJECT: I'M BACK (Attn: Basam)

Dear Basam,

GOD ALMIGHTY I've had a time. Here is what happened. The last time I e-mailed you was in the fall asking you for the address of Henrietta Gleason. I was meant to be attending the funeral of my ex-husband, victim of cancer, in October, but I ended up not going. It's a long story. Not long after that we had a hurricane and there was a power surge when lightning hit the transformer for my street and essentially the power surged all the way up into my very own electrical outlets and blew out my computer. It was a NIGHTMARE, it made an extraordinary pop and smoking, so I screamed and ran outdoors (humiliating). The entire computer had to be thrown away, not even worth the scrap, which was, as you can imagine, hell. I was under the impression that all of my e-mails were gone. All of my photographs and bookmarked websites, my library account. (As it turns out, I was able to retrieve most of this because it wasn't actually stored in the hard drive, but through the internet. There is a God.) But it's taken me months to get back up to speed, plus I've been in a knock-down, drag-out fight with the dean of the College of English at the University of Maryland, and on and on.
Did you try to send me your resume? I never got it.
Lastly, I've all but decided NOT to engage, but did you find the address for Henrietta Gleason? I apologize for the long silence.

Warm regards,
Sybil Van Antwerp

TO: sybilvanantwerp@aol.com
FROM: customerservice@kindredproject.org
DATE: Jan 6, 2016 07:07 PM
SUBJECT: Re: I'M BACK (Attn: Basam)

Dear Ms. Sybil Van Antwerp,

Thank you for contacting Kindred Project Customer Service! We are happy to help. Henrietta Gleason is not an active member of Kindredproject.org, and we cannot provide you with any personal information belonging to this individual other than what is available in the individual's profile if he or she reactivates his/her account.

Please don't hesitate to reach out with additional questions! Thank you for contacting Kindredproject.org.

Shelley

TO: customerservice@kindredproject.org
FROM: sybilvanantwerp@aol.com
DATE: Jan 8, 2016 10:07 AM
SUBJECT: Re: RE: I'M BACK (Attn: Basam)

Shelley, I would like this e-mail directed to Basam, the agent who handles all of my problems. I don't have his last name, but he's from Syria, married, two children, impressive engineering degree from Egypt. There can't be too many in your office with those specs.

Regards,
Ms. Van Antwerp

TO: sybilvanantwerp@aol.com
FROM: customerservice@kindredproject.org
DATE: Jan 8, 2016 09:12 PM
SUBJECT: Re: RE: RE: RE: I'M BACK (Attn: Basam)

Hello Ms. Van Antwerp,

Basam no longer works for Kindred. I would be happy to help you with any questions you have!

Please don't hesitate to reach out with additional questions! Thank you for contacting Kindredproject.org.

Shelley

TO: customerservice@kindredproject.org
FROM: sybilvanantwerp@aol.com
DATE: Jan 9, 2016 06:43 AM
SUBJECT: RE: Re: Re: RE: I'M BACK (Attn: Basam)

Hi Shelley, Well, where on God's earth has the man gone? Do you have a phone number or address, or an e-mail address, where I can reach him?

Ms. Van Antwerp

TO: sybilvanantwerp@aol.com

FROM: customerservice@kindredproject.org

DATE: Jan 11, 2016 04:44 PM

SUBJECT: RE: RE: Re: Re: RE: I'M BACK (Attn: Basam)

Hello, Ms. Van Antwerp,

I regret that I do not.

Please don't hesitate to reach out with additional questions! Thank you for contacting Kindredproject.org.

Shelley

Rosalie Van Antwerp
33 Orange Lane
Goshen, CT 06756

Dear Rosalie,

Get yourself a nice brandy and take a seat because I have a story
for you. I'm not joking now, Rosalie, pour the drink. Make sure
Paul and Lars are sorted.

    I fell. Please don't panic, I'm fine, but let me tell you the story.
About five days ago I couldn't sleep after I woke around four.
Typically I'll switch on the light by five to read, but I was lying in
the bed and feeling agitated. It was like I'd woken to a sound but
couldn't reach back to it. I lay there listening to the wind for a
while, and you know I just decided to go outside and be sure
everything was OK. The moon was bright and it was that crisp
February cold, so I put on a sweater and my coat, my boots, and
I walked outside. How strange it was to stand in the front yard
looking up into the tall trees, all their limbs moving shadows
like sticks under the moon, not a sound but the wind in the
leaves, and the garden I know so well felt like somewhere entirely foreign. Just beautiful. I wondered, have I ever come outside in the garden at this time of the morning in February?
Anyway, I decided to take the path down to the river and walk a
bit, you know, it was just so lovely, everything lit by moonlight. I
did go, and I walked for a while, and then I sat out by the river for
some time just thinking, really. You know, just pondering. My
age. The survey of my life thus far. My career, things I'd have
done differently (which for years I could not admit, and thinking
about why that is. Fear, I guess). I was thinking about the children, of course Gilbert, but moreover wondering what good
reason there is that I get on fine with Bruce but cannot seem to

have any sort of rapport with Fiona, you know. I sat for some time pondering things of this nature.

When I walked back up the path it was just barely getting light, maybe around six, and wouldn't you know Theodore Lübeck came down the path and scared me half to death, Rosalie. Not half, 80% of the way. I nearly died. He came from behind the magnolia that rather blocks the path wearing his cap and dark jacket and I screamed and jumped, and of course I tripped, went sideways on my ankle, which rolled and positively exploded in pain, and then I fell and caught myself on the right hand (mercifully not my left, God in heaven, can you imagine if I didn't have my left hand? Take me out back and shoot me). I felt it snap! I know you broke your foot in '94, wasn't it? But yours was crushed under that wheel, wasn't it? (Awful, I'm sorry, how vulgar) But my point is that my wrist snapped like a branch. It was no good, my ankle and my wrist just throbbing, and then Theodore coming barreling down the path, getting down on his hands and knees just like when I killed his cat (the humiliations keep coming) and begging my forgiveness and trying to help me to stand, which I did, cradling the hand, so of course he brought me back to my house (it was only another hundred yards or so, wasn't it, just there at the top of the hill) and he got me to the chair, and he was coming undone, trying to call 911 and I was chastising him, what a stupid fool thing to do calling the cavalry when one can simply get in the car, it's not as if I was bleeding out, but then I was in a bind because I knew the wrist was broken, and I knew I'd need Theodore Lübeck to drive me to the ER. So that's just what happened. He put me in <u>my own car</u> because he drives a very low to the ground old Porsche and he said it would be hard for me to get in and out (which I thought was rude, as if I would have trouble where he is fine!) and he took my own keys right from the hook and he drove me to the ER there in Annapolis. I was MORTIFIED, them assuming he was my husband at every turn, Rosalie. So they are examining me, you know, the ankle, the wrist, but also pressing on my stomach and listening to my lungs, making a whole to-do and it's not even time for coffee, I've got the night shift people, and I am howling like an idiot with none other than Theodore Lübeck sitting there, asking me if I want water, asking me if he should be calling the children to tell them (again, as if I'm dying and not suffering from a sprained ankle and broken wrist). I ended up in an X-ray machine and an MRI machine to confirm what I already knew, and then a surgeon came into the room to talk to me about the possibility of surgery on my wrist if the bones don't reset correctly. This surgeon turns out to be the son of a friend, Helen Dittmyer, and then we had to have the whole conversation about his mother, and on and on. Benji (now he's Dr. Dittmyer) also said my bones look strong for a woman of my vintage, and that made me feel great I'll say, but otherwise it was absolutely terrible. They put me in a splint that looks like something a child makes in art class, and now I'm home, and going back again in a few days for another X-ray and seeing what is to come. I dread if it's surgery. I do. It would be one or two nights in the hospital, and I imagine I would have to ask Bruce to come help me, which I would really rather not do, not wanting to mess up his life.

By the time we were back it was nearly two o'clock and I was starving, so we went through the drive-through at McDonald's and then we sat in the car eating the food, right there in my driveway. That was funny. Theodore was very good about the whole thing. He made me laugh. We were laughing about sitting there having lunch together for the first time out of bags in our laps. He mentioned a bit about his wife who did die rather young—sixty-eight. He has one daughter and she lives in California. I also learned that he is Jewish. I told him, all these years he's been bringing me Christmas gifts, and he said celebrates both holidays (he lights his menorah) but it was sweet I thought. And that's the whole story! It was nice with Theodore despite the circumstances. I will keep you posted on the wrist situation. My ankle is wrapped in a bandage I remove at night, but it will just have to heal. I'm using a cane for the moment, can you imagine? I refuse to use it beyond the weekend. I'll crawl on all fours if it comes to it.

Write me,

Syb

Feb. 29, 2016 (Leap year)

Dear Ms. Van Antwerp,

Thank you for the cherry streusel cake you had delivered from the German bakery in Baltimore. There was no need for you to go to the trouble, you have already thanked me multiple times, though it meant a great deal to me that you remembered that small thing I told you about my mother. I haven't thought in such detail about my mother in years, and I didn't know there was a German bakery until the cake showed up at my door. I was surprised to find it looking identical to my mother's, and tasting almost as good. I looked the bakery up in the phone book. The woman who answered, her grandmother started the shop when she came to Baltimore from Germany. She said her family is from the center of the country, whereas my family is from Küssaberg, just there at the very bottom, almost in Switzerland, but I told her the cakes were much the same, hers only a bit sweeter. She was glad to hear from me and we talked for a good while. She has never visited Germany. I think I will drive up to Baltimore and go to the shop so we can share a coffee and she can give me samples of other cakes and pastries she is trying to keep in the German style. She is a gentle sort of girl. That's the way Katharina, my wife, was. Quiet, though with Katharina there was always a bit of mischief. You'd see this little edge of a smile on her, made her look like she was so young, and even when she was completely vacant with dementia it was like that. Like the joke was on me.

It was also very nice to talk to you when we spent the morning together, though of course it was not good for you. Just as you seem determined to keep thanking me, I am determined to keep apologizing for startling you and setting things in motion. How are you getting along with the cast? I am relieved you don't have to have surgery. When I had surgery on my shoulder two years ago it was difficult for months in ways I didn't consider going into it, and I agree with something you said, that you dread dragging the children into your life when theirs seem busy enough already. You mentioned three children, but I think I've only met the two—Bruce and Fiona.

If you're not busy tonight, do you want to come play gin rummy? We can eat this cake. I also have a bottle of scotch, if you like. I rarely have company, but I've just dusted and mopped this morning. No need to let me know, just pop over around seven if you're free. If not, I'll drop a few slices of cake to you in the morning after my walk by the river.

This is the longest thank-you note I have ever penned. By the way, if I go to the German bakery, would you like to come? I estimate a thirty minute drive. We can talk about it if you come by tonight.

Your neighbor,

Theodore

Sybil Van Antwerp
17 Farney Rd.
Arnold, MD 21012

April 19, 2016

Dear Sybil,

I apologize that our conversation on the phone last week was cut so short on my end and that it's taken me this long to sit down to write. I did end up having to take Paul to the emergency room the next morning (it was pneumonia again). I had to ask a neighbor to sit with Lars, just complicated, but Paul's fine now and I had a full night of sleep and I'm here at last. Thank God the wrist business is almost behind you—cast off in a few more weeks—no surgery. That was the best case scenario. I just went and read over your letter from the week you fell and it made me laugh (now that I know you're all right). God, doesn't Mr. Lübeck sound like the most wonderful man? Honestly, Sybil. You know what I think, so I'm not going to keep saying it, but SYBIL. (This is unrelated, but I had a moment when I was reading the letter again thinking about all the letters we have exchanged—those boxes in my closet!—and thinking how if we pieced them back together we would have a MASSIVE decades-long tale to tell. Probably boring to anyone other than ourselves.)

I know you don't like me to bring up your vision, so typically I don't, but you mentioned it in your letter. What is the latest? When have you last seen Dr. Jameson? And here, speaking of your health, I know you were joking about the cane, but take your recovery seriously. You are very stubborn, and that is a wonderful quality except when it's not. I worry about you down there by yourself.

Now, another thing. In your letter you very briefly mentioned the strain in your relationship with Fiona, and while that wasn't the main point of your letter, I've thought a lot about it. I'm sure if

I had a daughter (or a standard child of any sex) it would be easier for me to relate, but I don't, and when you named Lars and me as Fiona's godparents, already knowing that I wouldn't ever have what you had, it was the greatest gift. I understood you were offering me an important, lifelong position and, as you know, I have always taken being her godmother very seriously. My relationship with Fiona is dear to me, and probably because I am <u>not</u> her mother she has felt, she feels, a strong connection to me without any of the tricky dynamics that always (inevitably, it seems) plague the relationships of mothers and daughters, and in fact, I have always had the feeling, even from the time she was a little girl, that Fiona knew she was providing me with something I could not otherwise have by allowing me to be a part of her life. I am exceedingly grateful to you for this gift.

Over the years there have been certain times when I have felt that I needed to pirouette between you and Fiona. I have a very strong allegiance to your family, but also to my individual relationships with you and with her. I have typically found a way to do this with what I think (I have tried) is integrity and honesty, respecting you both. However, after I read your letter I was moved to tell you something I kept from you.

After Daan passed away last fall Fiona came to visit me in Connecticut. She was having a very difficult time with everything and then a few weeks before Christmas she had to be in Boston for a work conference, so she added a few days to the trip and came to see me. It was a total surprise to me. She called the day before and asked if she could stop in, and I didn't realize until she was here that you didn't know she was in the US, and she asked me not to tell you. I agreed. (I regret this) We really just talked. That was all we did for two days, just sat on the porch out there and talked and talked, and it was Fiona doing most of the talking. She talked a lot about Daan's dying, and she was still in shock, very emotional, troubled by death in general, and still grieving all the agony of infertility, which I obviously under-stand, the years of negative pregnancy tests and the miscarriages she suffered before beginning IVF (I didn't know about any of it, and was surprised you hadn't told me), and she was just grap-pling with a great many things, one of which was her relation-ship with you. It isn't my place to disclose the details of the things she said, and I want you to know that I have always kept my loy-alty to you primarily, and I did then, too, but in the same way you are disappointed by the way it is with her, the same is true for Fiona, and it seems like an honest conversation might fix it. In your letter of May 25 you said you were pondering the reason for which you cannot seem to have a good relationship with Fiona. The thought of you losing sleep over this bothered me, and I re-membered you had told me she'd written you a mean note after Daan's funeral, mad you hadn't attended, and now I feel like I'm sitting on the sidelines when perhaps, by suggesting you deal with this issue head-on, my position between the two of you could actually be put to use. You both love each other.

All right then. I think that's all I wanted to say. I apologize for not telling you before now that she visited. Not telling you has made my stomach sour for the last six months and now I do imagine of course you will be hurt when you read this letter, so I am sorry. I'll wait to hear from you,

Rosalie

P.S. I am reading <u>Inferno</u>, the newest Dan Brown. What are you reading?

TO: sybilvanantwerp@aol.com
FROM: Mansourebas850@hotmail.com
DATE: May 22, 2016 05:13 PM
SUBJECT: This is Basam Mansour from Kindred

Hello, Ms. Van Antwerp,

I apologize for contacting you from my personal email address. I was let go from my position at Kindred before the new year, and now I am working as a driver for Uber and delivering carryout meals for a Vietnamese restaurant. I continue to look for work in my field.

I did something ignorant. I tried to send my resume to you from the customer service email address. There was a firewall in the system I did not know about, which screens attachments. It was foolish of me not to have predicted this. My supervisor did an audit of my emails and discovered the long history of exchanges we have shared. Finding my correspondence with you inappropriate, he cut off my access to client accounts and I worked for two weeks in a nonclient-facing role, and afterward was terminated. It was very bad, but I also understand and knew it was not ethical to do what I was doing: sending you my resume.

Several months ago I tried to email you. I received no reply and assumed you did not want to maintain communication outside of the Kindred context, understandably so, but this morning I returned to my email and evaluated the possibility I had spelled your email address wrong. I was working from memory, as I was not able to access any information in Kindred, as I said, once I was relocated in the company. And here was the problem! I'd spelled your name "von" rather than "van" initially.

If this is the correct email address, I hope you will reply, and please forgive me for this unconventional manner of communication. I am attaching my resume at last, and welcome your assistance if you have any to provide.

I hope to hear from you,
Basam Mansour

P.S. I did look into the account of the DNA match you had. I am forgetting the name, but I remember this woman who contacted you lives in Fort William, Scotland. When I worked for Kindred, I was troubled by the ethics of sending you this information, but I am free from that contract now.

Felix Stone
7 Rue de la Papillon
84220 Gordes
FRANCE

July 6, 2016

Dear Felix,

I have had such a week. I was going to call because it's too much to write, even for me, but you are on the hike in Argentina so it forces me to write it, which is better by far. Additionally, I had planned to spend this afternoon weeding the garden, but we've had a storm move in and it's looking like rain for the duration of daylight, so here I sit at the desk, and this gives me time to consider things as they come onto the page rather than simply prattling on and on and rushing through and tripping over my spoken words.

I have descended a spiral staircase to hell.

Ten days ago I received a letter from the <u>administrative assistant</u> to the dean of the College of English at UMDCP. SHE PAWNED ME OFF ON HER SECRETARY. This gal, her name is Ellie, said Melissa's position on the matter of my auditing an English course had not changed. In the last paragraph this woman (Ellie) said that Dr. Genet would very much appreciate it if I would "let the matter rest" as she has "already made her final decision." Let the matter rest I WILL NOT, <u>as you know very well</u>.

It was the very next day I received a phone call from James Landy. If you can't place the name, James was clerk to Tom Buggs, and then he went to the federal courts and now he's got his own bench. I have written letters back and forth with his son for almost ten years now, I guess, and the boy is troubled. His parents think he is demented in some way, but I have always thought they were misunderstanding. The child is a savant of mathematics. He is somewhat peculiar in social contexts, but so am I. His name is

Harry. He is charming, intelligent, thoughtful, but he has fits. He is treated poorly by the standard boys (athletic, cruel, you know the type; they were as bad to you). He is sixteen now, and the letters had begun to dry up, but I kept on, you see, rather having the sense that he was pulled on the one hand to quit writing to an old woman like myself, and on the other, to continue the letters as I believe it was rather a kind of therapy for him. He discloses his problems to me freely. Once a few years ago, I don't know if I ever told you this, he ran away and turned up on my doorstep, so you see what I'm saying is that we have a bond. Anyway, on top of this his mother is out of her wits. She was always an odd bird, but she's taken to stays in mental institutions over the last few years. It's an anxiety issue that apparently spread like kudzu. It just grew and grew and grew and then James called last week asking me when was the last I'd corresponded with Harry (it was around the holidays the last time I'd received a letter), so I told him, and he said that the boy tried to kill himself by taking pills. Would have done, too, but the maid found the child and called the ambulance and now he is in a hospital recovering and then he'll be moved to a mental place for rehabilitation for weeks or months. Oh, Felix. One does begin to feel very tired at times.

Mick Watts has invited me to come visit his home in Houston. He said he wants to take me shooting (imagine) and to his golf club for "the best crab cakes I've ever had"—in TEXAS—and I told him that was downright offensive. Anyway, he extended the invitation while we were speaking on the phone, and you know, Felix, I despise the notion of Texas with every atom in my being, a hot, barren wasteland of tumbleweed and people carrying guns and wearing cowboy boots, but I am actually considering the possibility. However, I'm in a quandary. How can I put this without sounding like an airless girl? I have been doing things with Theodore Lübeck. We have been playing gin rummy some evenings and we drove to Baltimore a few weeks ago to try a German bakery there called Oma's. We take walks on nice days together. I've not told Theodore about Mick, NOT that there is anything to tell, but when I received Mick's invitation I had a bad feeling in my bowels and I realized it's because after a quarter-century draught, at the age of seventy-seven, I find myself courted by two men at the same time!

Well, and here is the icing on the cake. This morning I log into my e-mail account on the computer and I'm surprised to discover a message from my good friend Basam. Do you remember that whole thing? He was helping me for a few years working with the Kindred website, he's a wonderful man, he is from Syria and he's an engineer, and I was going to try to help him find a decent job, and then last fall when the power surge took out my computer I was out of touch with him for several months and when I went back in the spring I e-mailed him and someone else at the company got back to me and said Basam no longer worked there. It was odd, you know, but so is life and that was that.

Lo and behold, an e-mail from Basam, from his PERSONAL e-mail address, in my e-mail account this morning just sitting there like a little rabbit with eyes up waiting for me. He was FIRED from Kindred because of the online correspondence he exchanged with ME (he tried to send me his résumé so I could find him a proper job), and anyway HERE IS THE THING (I am sorry, I told you it was too much to write, and I'm flying past details):

I have a DNA match. I've actually known this for some time, but what was I going to do with a thing like that? I'll tell you, I did nothing for quite some time. They didn't want me! Well, fine. But eventually curiosity got the best of me and I contacted this person (Henrietta Gleason is her name), but her account was suspended and I asked Basam to help me locate her, and that's just before the long stretch without communication came, and now he's back, and he grabbed some information for me before he'd left Kindred, and he said that the woman with whom I share 49% of my DNA lives in Scotland. Henrietta Gleason. What am I to do with that, or any of the above? Everything was going along without a single blip on the radar for years and BAM! CHAOS!

Call me when you're home
from Argentina,

Syb

Postscript: Fiona and I spoke on the phone this week—first actual call, not a text or e-mail, in a month—and she was calling to say they've successfully implanted another embryo and she'll have another baby. They know it's a girl because of science, and they're naming the child Frances, calling it Frannie. I swear I won't say this to anyone else, but I hate the name.

TO: sybilvanantwerp@aol.com
FROM: Roy@coastaleyepartners.com
DATE: July 20, 2016 8:23 AM
SUBJECT: Following up after your appointment

Dear Sybil,

It was great to see you yesterday, although as I said, the drops are not sustaining your vision as well as I'd hoped and the loss is happening more rapidly than we had hoped it would. Unfortunately, that's the nature of the beast. It can putter along for years, and then all of a sudden a fast decline. The gnats you see will get worse or stay stable, but it's unlikely they will go away, and the vision may begin to go in and out. Some days you may experience a dramatic vision loss in one or both eyes, and then the next day it could come back. It's no fun. I want to reiterate the point I made about my concerns with your living alone and the fact that you have not made your son and daughter aware of the situation. It won't be very much longer that I can, in good conscience, allow you to continue to drive, either. The last time you fell it was a bad result with your broken wrist, etc., but what if it's worse in the future? Stairs, a sidewalk curb? I wonder, could you hire some kind of companion or nurse for even some part of the days? I'm afraid with this sort of thing, one doesn't even always know the toll it is taking while the trouble is underway. The headaches you mentioned, too, are undoubtedly related to the strain on your eyes when you read and write, though I know you well enough by now to know you won't quit with that.

I really think you should contact the organization I mentioned, the Baltimore Services for the Blind. They've got good people and tons of resources for all the stages of this.

Also wanted to say thank you for the coffee table book of golf courses. It was very thoughtful of you, and completely unnecessary. You've given me a project—how many can I play? I'm forty-one. What's your bet?

Dr. Jameson

Sybil Van Antwerp
17 Farney Rd.
Arnold, MD 21012
USA

July 21, 2016

Sybil, we just got off the line and I'm sitting here chatting to Stew about the whole thing. As I think more about the matter of your little Miss Henrietta, I just can't help but think that it would be a shame if you knew you had a blood relation and you never contacted her—what a waste. And it wasn't her who gave you up, was it? She wasn't even born. You've uncovered a treasure! You can't just leave it flung out there.

Felix

TO: MDWattsIV@gmail.com

FROM: sybilvanantwerp@aol.com

DATE: Aug 19, 2016 8:23 AM

SUBJECT: Canceling visit

Greetings Mick, I'm writing with disappointing news. I will have to go back on my word after all and cancel next week's trip to Houston. A very dear friend is in something of a crisis at the moment and his teenage son is going to be staying with me here at the house for a little while. I'm not certain if it will be a few weeks or more, but certainly I will let you know. I've known the boy for years; his father is the honorable Judge James Landy, as a matter of fact. Did you ever cross paths? He's a lovely man, if a bit uptight and clinging to this modern Republicanism I've grown to despise. Anyway, I am sorry. I hope you can get your money back for the plane tickets. Of course as soon as I can, I'll be in touch. I am disappointed to miss the shooting.

Warm regards,

Sybil

Rosalie Van Antwerp
33 Orange Lane
Goshen, CT 06756

October 1, 2016

Dear Rosalie,

Harry has been here for just over two weeks. He got here looking awful, as gaunt as can be and dark circles under his eyes, his hair looking like he'd run a stick of butter through it, pimples all over his face. When James brought him to the door I nearly gasped. He's huge, as tall as Daan, but lean as a pole. It's painfully obvious the child is in need of a mother. He was about as limp as old lettuce and I could see James was holding his breath, hoping I wouldn't change my mind. James is positively thriving in his career, but wretched in the way of his family going to absolute shit. To hell in a handbasket, as they say. What a mess. There were tears in his eyes. He's blaming himself for the whole thing, and you know I don't blame him for all of it, but one does have to do a bit of self-reflection.

The boy is sullen for the main, and he does sleep a good deal, though James said this has to do with his medication and he used to run on five hours a night. He's got his schoolwork, but he stays on top of that on his own and I don't have to make him. He is funny about eating and he doesn't talk to me much. From his letters I'd assumed he would be more talkative, but either these past months have killed off something in him or all along he was finding confidence behind the veil of ink on the page, as many people do. He spends a lot of time upstairs in the bedroom. I think he is doing puzzles or reading (child loves puzzles and reading; he is obsessed with fantasy and science fiction) or he's on his computer a good deal. He plays World of Warcraft, which is a game about magic and battles. He also does coding, which he tried to explain to me, an exercise in futility. He goes out for a walk sometimes—I failed to mention he's brought his dog, a massive creature called Thor shedding hair I'm having to vacuum twice daily. He drives himself to therapy twice a week (Harry, not the dog). I don't think he's suicidal now. We have conversations about it. I ask him outright at least every other day. 'You won't try to kill yourself, then?' I want to make sure everything is very cut-and-dried, and he says he won't try it again and I believe him. He's a quirky child, but truthful. Very practical. I can usually get him to play a game or two with me in the evenings. He's sharp as a tack with cards and things. He's teaching me mah-jongg. We are watching a documentary series on a man who free-climbs steep rock faces. I'm trying to get a sense of what will motivate him. He's flat as a pancake. I'm glad he's here, though. You know, it makes me happy knowing he's here, and I guess that about answers your inquiry on how things are going.

It's hard to find time to write with a child in the house again, but I'll do my best. I'm still reading <u>The Round House</u> (Louise Erdrich).

Sybil

TO: Mansourebas850@hotmail.com
FROM: sybilvanantwerp@aol.com
DATE: Nov 11, 2016 08:21 PM
SUBJECT: Job + child in my house

Dear Basam,

Here is the update with my job search for you: I sent your resume to Dale Woodson via my son, Bruce. Bruce said Dale has been knee-deep in some terrific mess regarding a bridge that collapsed up in Pittsburgh (early morning, fortunately, only three people dead) and the state of Pennsylvania is suing the company that conducts safety checks. Anyway, Bruce is going to follow up with Dale in a few weeks when the dust of that proverbial wreckage settles (no pun intended).

Additionally, I wanted to fill you in on the latest. I mentioned to you I was going to be rather tied up because of hosting this teenage boy for a while. Well, as it happens he became very interested when I mentioned a bit about Kindred, the DNA testing, etc. I happened to mention to him about the match with Henrietta Gleason and Harry's face lit right up, saying that 49% is quite a match, absolutely sisters. That was a shock, but I kept my wits. He got onto the internet one evening when I was already asleep, and he found her. There was a notice in an online paper from the area about a local famous woman doing groundbreaking research in soil science named Henrietta "Hattie" Nell Gleason (She goes by "Hattie"). Harry followed some incomprehensible rabbit trail to find an address for her, indeed, as you remembered, in Fort William, Scotland. So now I am faced with this information and a decision has to be made. What do you think?

Warm regards,
Sybil Van Antwerp

December 26, 2016

Dear Theodore,

Thank you for the buckeyes you left on the doorstep yesterday, and a merry (and belated) Christmas to you, and a happy third day of Hanukkah as well. Everyone enjoyed the candies a great deal. Fiona didn't return home, and Bruce and his family only came for the day yesterday, so today I am tidying. I do apologize I wasn't able to attend the symphony performance with you in December. It appears Harry will be back up tomorrow or the day after, so then I'm back minding him.

When Harry gets back next week would you like to come have dinner and a game of Ticket to Ride?

Warm regards,

Sybil

(cont. Jan 2, 2017, previous pages UNSENT)

Each time the calendar rolls over to a new year, I become introspective. It's as if I am going into the pantry and surveying what is there, taking inventory—what I have, what's needed, the state of things. That's what I do every January first. So I spent the day thinking yesterday and one thing I decided was that I'm going to write to this woman in Scotland after all. You know I do believe in an intelligent God with plans and a firm grasp on what is happening down here—and if I'm meant to reach her, I will. At times it seems like insanity to trust in a thing like that. And yet I do. I must.

How strange my life has become recently. When Harry arrived in mid-September I'd assumed it would be for a few days or a week, and here we are these months later. He's coming back Sunday. Fiona's worried I'm being used; I am not. I've insisted he stay as long as it's the best thing for him. And now there is this Scottish woman with whom I am hoping to connect, one tiny little person out there in a sea of billions who is theoretically <u>my family</u>. How strange it all feels to me. I'm sitting at the desk this morning, it's fourteen degrees outside and snowing here and there, I'm all tucked in here with my tea and thinking about how strange it is, and wondering—have I been lonely? I wouldn't have ever said that, but now that I sit here thinking, I wonder, was I always lonely? I'm not sure I've ever felt at home in the world, but I'm not sure that's unique. I'm not sure. I'm really not sure what I sat down here to say, but it's like the whole neat thing has had a good shake and, for the first time in a long time, I have no idea what's around the corner.

Ms. Henrietta Gleason
Hoply
The Yule Road
Fort William PK98 4FC
Scotland
United Kingdom

January 6, 2017

Dear Ms. Gleason,

Please let me begin by saying this is far and away the strangest letter I've ever written, and I have written a number of letters. My name is Sybil Stone Van Antwerp and I was born in the United States on May 29, 1939, and adopted a little over a year after by Lawrence and Margaret Stone. I'd like to begin by saying that I never (never, never) meant to do something like this.

A few years ago at Christmas my oldest child, my son Bruce, gave me a gift of membership and DNA testing with an organization called Kindred. I believe his intent was twofold: his father (my ex-husband) was dying and he and his sister, Fiona, were facing that starkness of mortality and wanting to hold onto something, as we all do. Watching their father be erased with the incoming tide made them cling faster to me in a way, and that sense, I suppose, of one's lineage or history. In any case it took me some time to accept not only the gift but also the fact that there was something missing for them. I sent the saliva sample away at last. I was surprised by how anxious I became in waiting, an anxiety I couldn't define, and then the results came by mail. The pie chart of my alleged ancestry woke up something in me I hadn't even known was in slumber, a deep and hidden thing. I admit I wept over it. Do you wonder why I am sharing all of this with you? I rather do. Let me get to the point.

I never intended to open my DNA to the sharing option.

What I had gained in knowing my biological lineage threaded back to the British Isles, Russia, and Native Americans was plenty. It was a warm sense I had, even the vaguest, of roots. But there was a night when I was emotional, rather electric and outside my normal right mind, and it sounds mad, but by mistake I checked the box in the Kindred website to allow connections between my DNA and that of other users to be established. Before I knew it, within a week, I had an e-mail indicating Kindred had found a user with a 49% DNA match to me, and I am certain you know the direction of this, which is, namely and exclusively, that this person was, or, is, I believe, you.

For a number of reasons (not worth getting into) I didn't contact you initially, and then after a few months, I did. Immediately I received an error message from the website saying you were no longer a user. At the risk of frightening you, and in the interest of full disclosure, I admit I asked my friend who worked for Kindred to try and find your address (this was all happening over months, you see; I first learned of you in mid-2015) and then I lost communication with this individual, and I was of course putting a great deal of thought into these decisions. In due course I was able to sort out that you lived near Fort William, and then this month I've had a child staying with me, a disturbed boy who is the son of a friend, but he's extremely clever, you know, growing up in the age of the internet, and he found your address, and . . . VOILÀ.

My DNA matches your DNA by 49%. I know nothing about my biological family other than that I was adopted from inside the US. I was raised largely in Philadelphia.

I do hope you write, even if it's only a quick missive to tell me to bug off. It's just that now, this thing that has been woken, I can't seem to lull it back to sleep.

Warm regards,

Sybil Stone Van Antwerp

17 Farney Road
Arnold, Maryland
21012
USA

sybilvanantwerp@aol.com

Ms. Diana Gabaldon
8930 North Muir Circle
Scottsdale, AZ 85262

February 2, 2017

Dear Ms. Gabaldon,

I am writing to tell you I have just had the surprise of a lifetime
and that is, namely, reading your book, <u>Outlander</u>. Here is what
happened: I have two good friends, Trudy and Millie, whom I
have known for more than three decades and with whom I share
an ongoing discourse on literature. Our tastes do not always co-
incide; my preference is for modern literary fiction and nonfiction, and occasionally the classics of the 1800s to 1900s. Trudy
reads Christian fiction and historical fiction (specifically pertaining to the Revolutionary War, Civil War, and great World War
eras). Millie likes the classics best, but also some mainstream fiction and that is more whatever Oprah or Reese Witherspoon rec-
ommends, or what is on the table at Costco when she goes on
Thursday mornings. I'm getting too deep in the weeds. My point
is that I mentioned to the birds (those friends) that I was wanting
to read something regarding Scotland, particularly set up in the
Highlands, and Millie asked if I'd read your first book, <u>Outlander</u>.
I had not, and Trudy chimed in, rather blushing and echoing
back, yes, had I read it? They both had, though they didn't know
they both had and, in fact, they had both read all eight of the novels in your series, and I asked why neither of them had ever mentioned the series to me. Trudy was turning about as red as fresh
sunburn, but Millie (you'd love her, absolutely no shame whatsoever, she is from Long Island) looked me dead in the eyes and
said, THERE'S LOTS OF SEX. It wasn't the next day Trudy was
dropping her paperback copy at my front porch and I was finish-
ing another book (<u>Stoner</u> by John Williams, a third read for me),
so it was perfect timing and I tucked right in.

Well. I read all day, skipped garden club, read into the night, woke in the morning, and read all the next morning, finished the book the weight of a doorstop that night and stepped onto my back porch like an opossum blinking blearily. "Lots of sex," as it turns out, was understated, and I'll not pretend I didn't enjoy it, though there were some of the violent bits I admit I skipped over, my word. But it was the PLACE. From the comfort of my reading chair, my feet on the ottoman, the light on at my head, my tea, I've been positively delivered into the interior of Scotland. How can I thank you? And the history, too, and the wonderful characters, and the storytelling I loved. I loved the book, AND, as it turns out, I have a special connection to Fort William discovered rather recently, which made the history the more interesting to me. The character of Claire was very relatable to me (I am rather an unfiltered person). It was such a pleasant surprise, and still seven books to go!

Will you continue to add to the series? Are you a historian? You seem to know such a great deal about the history of Scotland and the dynamics with England. It makes you rather hate the British does it not? And did you begin as a writer or a historian? I'd love to hear from you, if you are the letter-writing sort. Most are not, but every once in a while I strike oil.

Warm regards,

Sybil Van Antwerp

Mr. George Lucas

℅ LucasFilm Ltd.

Letterman Digital Arts Center

1 Letterman Dr.

Presidio of San Francisco, CA 94129

February 24, 2017

Dear Mr. Lucas,

I hope this letter finds you in good health. Typically when writing a letter to a celebrity I have a great deal to say, but in this case I find myself at a bit of a disadvantage because I have never seen the Star Wars movies. I feel foolish here, knowing they are an American institution, it's just that I rarely watch television and I don't enjoy science fiction, but I'm sure your work is very, very good to have rendered you so extremely successful.

I am crossing my fingers that your staff has passed along this message in a bottle I am rather chucking into the Pacific. I am an old woman and I find myself in a strange situation of hosting a high school-aged boy at my house for a few months. This child is extremely intelligent, but he is deeply sad. He is not my grandson, but you might assume he was if you saw us together. He has come to stay with me in order to convalesce from a suicide attempt (I hope you will keep this sensitive information in confidence), but he is VERY clever. He's been accepted to Stanford, the Massachusetts Institute of Technology, Harvard, and maybe someplace else, and these acceptances are to do with his comprehension in mathematics, I believe.

Getting to my reason for writing: Over the past few years Harry has been working on a book. As a matter of fact, I think it's more like he's been working on creating a world—there are notebooks upon notebooks of information. He has begun to weave it all together into a story and just this week the boy passed me about 140 pages of material. I was astounded. I knew he wrote stories, but I didn't have any idea the scope of the endeavor. It's <u>very good</u>, remarkably creative, and with a powerful quality of intrigue really from the first page. Tremendous. Not being a creative myself, I have nothing to contribute, but I thought of you. I read an interview you gave several years ago and you seemed lovely, just a regular man talking about raising your children. I've always remembered that, and so I thought I would reach out and see if you might simply write to Harry. He idolizes your work. Give him a bit of encouragement to keep on with it, you know. It would be wonderful if you would do that for him (without, of course, it goes without saying, mentioning that I told you he tried to kill himself).

Harry (Landy is his surname) will be here with me until summer, or you can write to him at his home:

98 Dumbarton St. NW
Washington, DC 20007

Thank you very much for your consideration, and with warm regards I write,

Sybil Van Antwerp

TO: sybilvanantwerp@aol.com
FROM: jameswlandy@gmail.com
DATE: Mar 3, 2017 05:25 AM
SUBJECT: Marly

Sybil,

Thank you for having me up for dinner last night. It was very nice to see the way Harry's demeanor has relaxed since he has been stay-ing with you.

I wanted to follow up on a few things. If you do not cash the checks I've sent, I'll bring him home. It's enough you're keeping him and I'm not going to allow it to be a financial responsibility on top of the rest. I'll keep sending a check each month, the amount being my own prerogative. I don't care what you do with the money; I know you don't "need" it. Maybe you should get a new roof; yours looks in need of replacement. Buy a sailboat. Plan a trip to Italy. Get some-one in there to build you bookshelves in that sunroom.

It was never my intention to leave Harry this long with you, and I know it can't go on like this forever, but now that I have Marly at home, it's a full-time job. She is agitated and cries all the time or erupts in anger or sleeps for a whole day. She wanders in the house at night. Don't think I'm sleeping, but can't be sure. It's unbearable, and yet, every time I see Harry he seems better, more content, more at ease, and you continue to emphasize you don't mind having him, so I'm inclined to let him stay (which is what he wants). At this point the school year only has a little longer and the school said he can complete the year in this hybrid remote capacity. Are you sure you don't mind? I will plan to bring Harry home come summer (mid-May), if it's alright with you.

And lastly, I'd say Theodore Lübeck is in love with you. What an interesting man. Do you know the details surrounding his family leaving Germany? I will say, he is a funny sort. The way he's dressed like it's still 1978, and that European hat of his, but he's smart and interested in everything you say. I'm certain he's in love with you, but it's my understanding from Harry that you are involved with a retired attorney from Texas.

I'm taking Harry to California to visit Stanford again before he makes his final decision. I have been hoping he would stay on the East Coast, but he seems most drawn to Stanford. I'll take him out in a couple weeks, leaving that Thursday, March 16.

Thanks for the flowers you cut for Marly. She loved them. Your garden looks like something out of a magazine about the English countryside truly. Talk soon—James

The flowers were all decapitated. Every bloom and bud snipped and left on the ground. Harry was out early to take the dog to the bathroom and he came running back inside. When I stepped out, everything was green, a monotone jungle, but the blooms littered the ground like the candy from a piñata. We went around and collected them, then tossed them in the bin. Without stems one cannot even put them in glasses. I felt numb. Rather, I felt resigned to the inevitable.

My neighbor Theodore, himself something of a gardener, came by shortly later, knocking on the door, upset by the obvious massacre, and so with Harry and Theodore in the kitchen asking questions it came out about the notes I have received from the angry individual with the initials "DM." It had been quite some time since the last one, so I'd thought perhaps it was over. I told them it was someone needling me from back in the courthouse days, but I couldn't bear to show them the notes, so I said I'd thrown them out (though of course I have not). Theodore said he was going to call the police, but I would not let him. Cutting flowers from their stems is no crime; it's only April and many of the bushes will bloom again. What evidence do I have but the letters, which I could not bear to show them.

My houseguest Harry is different, though. He is fortunate to lack a certain civilized propriety that makes the standard person self-censor. He continued asking questions later that evening. I feel a certain openness with Harry. We are alike. We also have an established commitment to discreet confidence with one another. I showed him the notes. He studied them quietly for some time and the first question he asked me was if I knew who DM was. I said I thought I probably did know. There are some cases that stay with me, and one in particular, and it— Oh, Colt. If I could rewind the clock—do certain things differently. I have really made such a mess of things. He watched me for some time and after a bit Harry got up and ran me a glass of cold water. He set it down on the table and then he went to the drawer beneath the phone and took a slip of notepaper and a pencil and set them down in front of me, too. I wrote out the name and the date of the case and he asked me what I needed. Enzo Martinelli. I can still see him. I said an address would be sufficient. I went to bed, and in the morning there was a list of options he had found, so now I have it.

Oh, Colt.

TO: sybilvanantwerp@aol.com
FROM: debbakescakes@yahoo.com
DATE: Apr 28, 2017 08:10 AM
SUBJECT: Your Garden Club Office Position

Good afternoon, Sybil:

Due to the fact that you have missed the past three meetings of the Severn River Garden Club, in addition to the leadership meeting preceding the general meeting last week, the leadership has agreed to remove you from the position of club secretary effective immediately. I have my own duties as name badge chair, but I offered to take over your duties, so you can send me your most current membership list Excel spreadsheet. I will order you a new general membership name badge, so you can dispose of your badge with the gold rim that says "Secretary."

Sincerely,
Debbie Banks

TO: grandmaalicelivingston@yahoo.com
FROM: sybilvanantwerp@aol.com
DATE: Apr 28, 2017 10:49 AM
SUBJECT: Overthrown

Alice, well, of course this was going to happen all along. Looking back, I do see it now. Debbie Banks is a formidable woman, and wasn't she looking for a chink in my armor for YEARS? I suppose she has found it, and that is fine by me. She can have the position. I'm not sorry for my absence. As I told you, I have had a long-term houseguest since the fall and garden club happens to fall at a time in the evening when the fish are biting. My guest likes to fish in the evening before dinner and frankly I enjoy his company far more than I enjoy our meetings, which have become overrun with women more interested in chattering on about their bygone husbands, arthritic joints, and bowel movements, and munching on cakes and cookies than information about gardening. I hope you don't feel the need to step down from your own position as treasurer out of loyalty to me; Stay! You have Mary in the club, anyway. If I had a daughter-in-law attending, I'd probably be on my best behavior. (Well, probably not, but I will say if I had a daughter nearby I'd be with her every chance I had.)

Sybil

Sybil Van Antwerp
17 Farney Rd.
Arnold, MD 21012

May 16, 2017

Dear Sybil,

It's been a while since I have heard from you, either letter or phone, and what communication we have exchanged has been brief. I know you're very busy with Harry in the house and the mess you have with the garden club, but my life is small and boring! I miss our correspondence. Is everything OK?

Paul's back surgery is scheduled for the first week of June, and as much as I am dreading it, I wish it would just go ahead and get here so we could move on. The recovery will be difficult, but in the long term, theoretically, it will ease some of his ongoing discomfort. With that on the horizon, and the physical intensity of caring for him, I've been debating more and more the nursing home for Lars. My right shoulder is weakening from lifting Paul, and I just went to see a doctor who thinks I need to have shots for the pain in my back. Anyway, I went and took a tour of Greenmont Village and had a meeting with the director, who seems very smart and caring. She can't believe I haven't acted sooner, but everyone says that. If I was outside the situation I'm sure I would be saying of course, put him in a home, but it feels different from inside the situation. It is so strange now that we are here (Lars and me), now that it is us, with all the memories we have. From the outside I'm sure he looks like a brainless slug, but he is my partner. Putting him in a home feels like surrendering. Like I'll be giving all that up.

In other news, you'll be happy to know I've been cleaning out my closet and drawers, going through and taking out things I'll never wear again, and giving them to Goodwill. As a treat to myself, I drove an hour to Nordstrom last week when I had the nurse here for most of the day. A really nice sales gal helped me pick two pairs of comfortable slacks, a pair of jeans, one new dress, and some cute sneakers meant to be worn casually, not for exercise. It was fun.

Did you ever hear back from the letter you wrote to your relation in Scotland? And how are things going with Mick? I am reading The World Below by Sue Miller. What are you reading?

Love,

Rosalie

Dear Sybil,

Happy birthday. I hope you are able to enjoy it, and you aren't worrying. I am worried about you and I wish you would let me engage some kind of investigator. I keep my eyes peeled. I'm sticking to my word, and now I will tell you why this date holds significance to me, a story I have rarely had reason to retell. I remember you saying you find it is easier at times to write than it is to speak. What happened on 29 May 1941 brings me both grief and shame, although with age I have learned my feelings and my experience are, sadly, not unique. Terrible things happen. We make choices. Time cannot be rewound. The good that comes out of the bad can be unbearable.

My father was in denial about the situation for Jews even though, as Americans say, the writing was on the wall. He forbade talk of it at the dinner table. He was always laughing too loudly when the rest of the village had become somber. He did not want to accept what it was to be Jewish under the Nazis, but then a man my father worked with disappeared. His name was Levi Holtz. Holtz was also a Jew, and it was one day my father was supposed to meet him to look at making repairs to a building on the edge of the town, and the man didn't arrive. My father called up to his house and the housekeeper answered. She said when she had arrived in the morning to work there was not anyone there but the dog trapped in the larder. That was when my father had to remove his head from the sand. He snapped into action and made some calls. He found us passage out of Germany and set it for the end of May. My father was friendly with everyone—Jews and Christians, no matter, always the life of the party and smiling and saying yes because it was good for business, obedient to the new rules and friendly with the Nazis, thinking if he behaved they would treat us better. He'd built houses or buildings and things for so many people, and he was well liked because he only ever said the things people wanted to hear. He taught me that, too. To say what people want to hear, not necessarily the truth, because most people tell you they want to hear the truth, but they do not, and if you tell the truth it will come back to bite you like a snake finding its own tail to swallow. I remember how he would say this to my brother and me and I didn't like the way it sounded because my mother taught the opposite, that if we do not say the truth we have nothing. We are nothing.

When Holtz disappeared, my father found us a way to leave, and the date we would leave was 29 May. A car came to the house in the early morning, maybe four. We had two suitcases and a few small bags. My father locked the front door as if we were leaving on a holiday, but I had seen my mother packing strange things like the paperwork of our births and a locket from her sister she never wore, so in that way there was no pretending. My brother, my mother, my father, and I climbed in and we drove. The morning was heavy with cold fog when the sun began to rise. We drove in silence and it was a young woman driving, younger than my mother, and I thought she was a man at first because her hair was cut short and she wore a man's cap. My mother was thirty-one. This girl drove us out of town in a direction I had never been on small roads. We went up into some hills and then the girl pulled up in front of a house beside a lake and there was a mill there and another car running. And what happened is that we all of us got out of the car and a man stepped from the driver's seat of the other car and he looked at us and he looked at the girl who had delivered us. He said he would take one adult and one child, no bags. My father had been cheated. He had paid for four of us to get out, but at some exchange of hands the money was only enough for two. I have lived a long life. I am eighty-one now and when I look back here is the worst moment, when I was not six years old. My father wept, disbelieving, and begged the man to take all four of us, but the man said we had to go without delay and he would take one adult and one child only. At this, my mother fell to the ground. She clawed at the man, asking him to take my brother and me. It was embarrassing to me when I was a boy that my mother was on the ground like an animal, her blouse coming untucked. For many years I thought of this man as worse than the devil himself until I was grown and married and had my daughter. Then I still hated him but could finally understand. I wonder how many people he drove to asylum. I do not know his name or any other detail. He said one adult and one child now, or he was leaving. My mother stood and composed herself and took a few things from the bag and tucked them into her pockets and she put me in the car. Although I understood what it meant I did not fight because I wanted to escape. There was another woman in the front seat and a teenage girl with her hair set in curls in the back already. My mother kissed my father and my brother, who was five years older than me, goodbye and got in after me. She was silent and her hair was messed and her white blouse dirty from the ground. My brother stood beside my father and the girl who looked like a boy. My brother was very quiet and still, but my father stumbled after the car as we drove away. Mother stared out the window the whole way. We drove for hours. We changed cars again. We did not speak. We went into Switzerland. My father and my brother went to Dachau and died there. They shared the name Joh. I remember a time my mother was vibrant, honest, beautiful, but all of it was extinguished. I wish I would have spoken up to offer my brother safe passage, but I did not. I was only a child. I was learning what vastness is found in the hearts of men.

You were right when you said that sometimes writing something difficult is easier.

Every year the anniversary of that day comes and I grieve. I cut flowers to put in a vase in memory of my brother and my father, but also I cut roses for the celebration of your birthday, which makes me glad. I feel fortunate we have become friends the last couple of years. I had reached a point of thinking my life had run out of surprises.

Tracey said this cake was the best one they make at the bakery, good for breakfast or dessert. I hope you enjoy it.

Yours,

Theodore

Felix Stone
7 Rue de la Papillon
84220 Gordes
FRANCE

May 31, 2017

Dear Felix,

Harry's left. I don't know what I was doing with myself before. How did I fill the days? Reading, letter writing? Is that all it was? I had begun to look forward to having my life back to its old order, but now that he's gone the quiet feels like loneliness, where it did not before. At least, if it did, I didn't realize. There is a half-complete 2,000 piece jigsaw puzzle on the formal dining table. It's not quite so fun without Harry. I'll probably put it away.

Anyway, Mick Watts is back to inviting me down to Texas, and I've run out of excuses, so I have said I'll go. I leave June 16 and I'll be gone a week. I'm flying, which I dread, but Trudy and Millie (who love the idea of Mick, though they haven't met him obviously) are going to come help me pack my things and take me to the airport. It's a direct flight from Baltimore to Houston, and Mick said he will meet me at the airport. I wonder, Felix, why he wants me to come so badly, an old dog like me. Surely there is a queue of (younger) women vying for his bachelor attention and his money.

Please send along your dates for November so I can clear my schedule. You can, of course, borrow the car. I haven't told you this, but I'm not driving much. I get a ride with the birds or my neighbor Theodore for the most part.

Your loving (seventy-eight-year-old) sister,

Syb

Rosalie Van Antwerp
33 Orange Lane
Goshen, CT 06756

June 5, 2017

Hello, Rosalie. I am writing because I know Paul's surgery is Friday. I hope you have prepared well in advance, and have some kind of assistance with care lined up. To answer your questions, Harry has left, I have not heard from the DNA relation in Scotland, and things are going along fine with Mick Watts. I am reading <u>To the Lighthouse</u> by Virginia Woolf.

And lastly, you asked if everything is all right. No, everything is not all right. I cannot quite manage to move past the fact that you, my best friend, the person I held dearest to myself, would betray me by hosting my own daughter, who, as you very well know, I see once a year if I am lucky, and <u>keep it from me</u>. How humiliating, that you and she should see fit to need to conduct clandestine meetings. How wonderful it must be for you to have such a strong bond with Fiona, such an intimate, confiding relationship. I cannot imagine such a pleasure, but it sounds WONDERFUL. I just relish the thought of her cozying up in your den telling you all the ways in which I have failed her as a mother, and how glad she is to have a surrogate in you. I hate to think how bereft she would be if not for you, Rosalie.

You and I have enjoyed an honest, confrontational friendship for going on sixty years, and I cherished it. Good luck with Paul next week. In all hope, it'll go smoothly for him.

Sybil

Postscript: For your information, before the letter in which you confessed to your little surprise reunion behind my back I was unaware of Fiona's troubles with infertility and miscarriages, so thank you for providing me with that information.

Sybil Van Antwerp Stone
17 Farney Road
Arnold
MD 21012
United States of America

11 June 2017

Greetings, Sybil,

I received your letter from January at the end of April. The letter went to an old address, then it seems it went round and round never finding its way and finally it did come to me all bent and rumpled as if it'd been shoved someplace. I kept the letter to myself for several days and read it repeatedly, so many times the paper began to soften, stunned so I was. When I started with Kindred it was to trace familial lines of my father, an American, about whom I have very little knowledge, and when they began the DNA testing it was offered to me free of charge, so I did it rather without much thought, I'm somewhat embarrassed to say, seems a bit foolish, doesn't it? And anyway, shortly after it I was going through some bills and trying to tidy up and cut back (I'd really already got as much information as I could about my paternal lineage), so I printed out the family history I'd found and closed the account. Hadn't given Kindred a thought again until I read your letter.

I am a botanist, familiar with DNA. Initially, I thought the letter had to be some kind of hoax. A 49% match is absurdly high, and with you materialising from thin air it was something I couldn't believe. And yet there was your pristine penmanship on the cream paper, the names of your children. There is no other way to say it: I believed you. I took your letter down to my brother, who runs the pub and a hardware store and we mulled it over for a while. (This was after weeks.) Then I was down in Glasgow teaching a summer course at university, and turning this over and over again in my mind all the time, and now I'm back and made it my first task on returning to my house to write.

I was born in October of 1943, and my brother Declan the year after me. John and Douglas are twins, and were born in 1948. Would you please, if it isn't a bother, send along a copy of the report of our DNA match? Please don't take it as rudeness, it's only I feel the need to see it with my own eyes.

If you will, please send to my correct address, and that is

Hattie Gleason

Bodney Cottage

Fassfern

Fort William PH33 7NP

Scotland

My apologies for the long wait. I won't take so long the next time, and hope you won't punish me by waiting your own six months to reply. I'm on the edge of my seat, as they say. You yourself, Sybil, open a door to a world of possibility.

Very best wishes,

Hattie

TO: MansoureeeBas850@hotmail.com
FROM: sybilvanantwerp@aol.com
DATE: Jun 26, 2017 10:15 AM
SUBJECT: SHE WROTE

Dear Basam, Hattie Gleason has written me AT LAST, as I live and breathe. It arrived at my house the same day as myself after a trip. (I went to Texas to spend a week with a man.) She is a botanist living in Scotland. She has brothers named Declan, John, and Douglas. She is four years younger than me. She wants to see a copy of the DNA match. (Of course she does. It was IDIOTIC I didn't send it along with my letter, but perhaps I was feeling wary, as well, of sending off something so personal, but anyway, I will send the document to her. All the personal information it lists she has—my name, birthday. And, of course, the months I've waited for a letter in the mailbox from her, I've thought it must be a terrible shock. It was a terrible shock to me! Perhaps one doesn't welcome shocks of this kind, necessarily. Perhaps she'd burned the letter, or thrown it away thinking it was a scam. It certainly seems like a scam. A "hoax" is the word she used.)

She said I have pristine penmanship, which is true. It's unfortunate our entire correspondence has been through the e-mails so you have never seen it. I rather feel the way I write e-mails is less thoughtful than written letters. I'll have to mull on that, another day.

I'm absolutely frantic, happy, nervous, buzzy. It'll be time to clue in my brother, Felix, now, I suppose. Or maybe not. Maybe my girlfriends, but no. They will want to participate in the letter writing. I may tell my neighbor. He's a gentle sort, a good listener.

Fill me in on your life.

Sybil

Ms. Sybil Van Antwerp
17 Farney Rd.
Arnold, MD 21012

July 18, 2017

Dear Ms. Van Antwerp,

There is a movie coming out this month and I saw the trailer and it made me think of you. It's about an old woman who lives alone like a hermit. She is eccentric and rude, but you come to find out that she used to be the personal assistant to a United States president (I'm not sure if the movie supposes an actual previous president, like Kennedy or something, or if he's fictional), and then it looks like maybe she was a Russian spy or something.

I am excited that Hattie Gleason wrote to you. Did you ever write the letter to Dezi Martinelli? If you did, did he write you back? Did Melissa Genet let you audit an English class?

My dad put the note George Lucas sent me in a frame and it's on my desk.

Warm regards,

Harry Landy

Mr. Harry Landy
98 Dumbarton St. NW
Washington, DC 20007

August 1, 2017

Dear Harry,

Thank you for your letter. The movie sounds interesting. I have not written the letter you suggested. I understand this letter falls out of date, but it looks like you have abandoned the letter-writing schedule that we have previously kept, and that is helpful because it was necessary I write you today. I will pick you up on Thursday next, August 10, and together we'll go see Melissa Genet. Please tell your father I'm taking you to the Smithsonian and to lunch as a send-off for university. I hope you don't feel like you're being used, although I suppose that's exactly what's happening. I'll be outside your house promptly at 9 am. Please be ready to go, and looking decent, not in gym shorts or a t-shirt with images on it. I think khaki shorts, since it's going to be over a hundred degrees Thursday, and a nice polo shirt. Make sure, Harry, make sure you comb your hair and brush your teeth.

I'll see you then. Not a word to your father.

Ms. Van Antwerp

Postscript: The vision declines. Do you think my penmanship is worsening?

Sybil Van Antwerp
17 Farney Rd.
Arnold, MD 21012

August 20, 2017

Oh, Sybil. I have plenty to say to you and I plan to say every bit of it with the understanding that once you've read it I won't expect to hear from you for a while. July and August have been very full for me, which is partially why I haven't replied to your (ugly) note, but the fact is that I also needed time to think about what I wanted to be sure to say.

It was obvious you were still angry Fiona had visited me even though you said you were fine, and I tried to give you space to let it go, but clearly you didn't. I have apologized to you once already for keeping it from you and I meant that apology, but I'm not going to apologize again. What is more, I am not going to apologize for things I would do over again without a second thought.

When Fiona came to see me the Christmas after Daan died she was very upset. She arrived at the house and her face was gaunt, her eyes were gray, her hair flat and the roots growing in. She looked totally unlike herself, and when she saw me, Sybil, she fell apart. I thought something horrible had happened, like Walt had cheated on her or she'd embezzled money or something truly capable of destroying her life, that is how bad she seemed when she came to my house. As I've explained already, I didn't know she was coming until she showed up. It isn't as if Fiona and I regularly chat on the phone or meet up. I'm irritated that I feel the need to report to you on this, but at this point it's obviously necessary. Fiona emails me or texts me every so often, and I her, and of course I send cards on holidays and birthdays, and every once in a while we'll catch up on the phone, but it'd been a while. I think we had texted around Daan's funeral, and that was all, so I was shocked at her sudden appearance (I had not seen her in person in more than five years I don't think) and in such a bad state. I'm not sure if you are aware of how Daan's death shook Fiona, and of course after your last letter I am hesitant to inform you of anything you don't know, but she was deeply, disturbingly grieved. As a matter of fact, the intensity of her grief reminded me of you when Gilbert died. It was wild grief. As she started to talk through her sadness a lot of what she told me pertained to her relationship with you or, frankly, Sybil, the lack thereof.

Even though it is not my place to tell you this, I'm going to. Fiona was hurt that you had not attended Daan's funeral, yes, but over the course of her visit she seemed to be digging down and uncovering deeper stores of anger toward you from throughout her life. I want you to know that most of what I did was listen, and when I did speak it was mostly in defense of you, but I was not, I am not, able to speak on your behalf. Of course I defended you, you're my best friend, but I did not feel it was my place to explain certain things, specifically things about Gilbert's death, even though I found myself recalling vivid memories of that horrible day and the days that followed, and thinking over and over again how you just needed to have an honest conversation with each other, for her to lay out her feelings and give you time to respond, to help her understand. She is selfish—of course she is! We were all selfish at that age, weren't we? And she has no idea what losing Gilbert did to you, what the divorce did to you because you have never told her! For reasons I don't fully understand, you have pushed Fiona away from yourself, Sybil. Why have you? What is clear to me, what you are somehow blind to see, is that if you would step toward Fiona you could fix this. Fiona does not need me, she needs you! Step toward Fiona and be the mother she needs. You are a wonderful, interesting woman, full of love and kindness, but you are so damn stubborn and determined you know exactly what is right in every situation. I am willing to sacrifice all that I have with you, my dearest friend, if it means opening your eyes to salvage what you can have with Fiona. Fix it, Sybil. Fix what is broken.

Now, like I said, I won't expect to hear from you after this, but I want to end by reminding you that I love you. I wish I had not been the one to tell you about Fiona's miscarriages; I'm sure that was a painful thing to swallow. And Paul's surgery did not go smoothly, it was about six weeks of pure hell, but I do feel that we have turned a corner.

Rosalie

D. Martinelli
138 South Carrington St.
Hasbrouck Heights, NJ 07604

September 6, 2017

To Dezi,

Whatever it is you feel the need to say to me, I invite you to go ahead and say it. You can write me at this address, or by e-mail. My hope is that by offering you the chance to say your piece, you will do so and then you will leave me alone.

Regards,

Sybil Van Antwerp
sybilvanantwerp@aol.com

Felix Stone
7 Rue de la Papillon
84220 Gordes
FRANCE

October 3, 2017

Dear Felix,

I'm sorry I haven't been in touch. My head has been off somewhere else, I guess. Things have been a bit busy lately, but it was lovely to hear from you, as always, and I can't believe I haven't filled you in about the latest development with the UMDCP English fiasco. You will think I've completely lost my mind.

There is no other way to put this, Felix, but something got into me. I took Harry and I showed up at the College of English in College Park. It was a Thursday, and I knew she would be there that morning because Harry, with his internet savvy, had discovered a calendar of the department and there was to be a department meeting at 10:30 am, ninety minutes. You know the way I can be when I get my mind on something, so I left Harry under a tree by the car and I planted myself outside of the room where the meeting was being held.

They all came filing out of the room chattering away and carrying little styrofoam cups of coffee and nobody noticed me. (This is the trouble with being only five foot one inch, and it has always been the trouble, but you know I am tall on the inside.) I did see two professors I've audited in the past, but I kept my gaze averted and I didn't see Melissa. I knew what she looked like because Harry had shown me her photo on the website as well as the press release from when she'd been hired, and I was looking for her, no luck, but you know, this thing had gotten into me. I went into the conference room when the trickle of English department staff or what have you had slowed to nothing and I saw her. Felix, she is shorter than me! I couldn't believe it. The tiniest little woman in black slacks and a gorgeous yellow wool cardigan sized for a twelve-year-old, I'm telling you. (I guess she was wearing the heavy sweater because it was absolutely freezing in the building, something men do in summer, turning women to popsicles.) Anyway, I stood in the back and waited for her to finish the conversation she was having with a man (a monstrous man in his fifties, large gut, red face, and Melissa is this tiny and absolutely gorgeous black woman maybe forty years old with long braids I don't know how she could stand under the weight of them! Amazing, and this man was speaking down to her both literally and figuratively and I could see there was that quality in her eyes—you know what I mean. Defeat.). She didn't see me there, and even when this man left she didn't notice me. I had marched my way into the building ready for a fight, but I could see that she was upset or weary, this very small woman, and my hackles went right down.

I said excuse me, and she was surprised the room wasn't empty, I could see. She was wearing these lovely earrings. They were feathers. As I mentioned, she is a very pretty woman, but she looked positively haggard. Wilted as a rotten peach. A bit of lipstick would have done wonders. I told her who I was, and rather still prepared for a duel, I stood up as tall as I could and it was one of those auditorium seating theaters so I had that advantage of being at the top, and it took her a moment to place me, so I told her I was the woman who'd been fighting to audit courses for two years. She looked positively surprised and we faced off for another moment, but then all the air went out of it, and it seemed very funny to me all of a sudden. I don't know what on earth was happening, but I found myself trying not to smile, or rather, trying not to laugh, but my face must have broken and then we were both laughing, these two short women standing thirty feet apart, it was really very funny. And so I asked her if she wanted to have a coffee, and she said she would prefer wine, so I said that was fine, I would go for a glass of wine (it was noon, after all) but then I remembered that young Harry was at the car, so I told her I had this friend with me, and she said she didn't mind, she'd be glad to have this friend along, so we walked to her office (which was absolutely littered with papers and books and only has this one small window—she's the DEAN, for the love of the world) and she took her sunglasses and dropped off her sweater. She was wearing a green t-shirt and she had these thin little arms, she is very fit, but thin, and I had the thought I should bring her home with me, feed her, let her sleep off some of the misery I saw in her face. We went for the wine at a patio near the campus (Harry had a Coke). In the end she told me she didn't care a shred. I could audit every class if I wanted to, that she was trying to establish her authority, but it wasn't going easily. She's had a hell of a time, at her age, and she is treated poorly—you know, Felix, people are downright racist and sexist—and she said that being a poet, she isn't taken seriously. She said that's what it was that first put her off me—I'd mentioned a disinterest in poetry (and I really do dislike most poetry, but I could see why she might be defensive), but I told her she was going to have to grow some thicker skin, and I told her about my time working for Donnelly, the fortifications I had to learn being an alien (female) in a world of men, though of course for me, a white woman, it was not nearly so large a mountain as the one she is endeavoring to climb, and it was all in all a very good conversation. So that was that, and I'm sitting in a class on the Brontës this term. It meets Wednesdays at 1pm. It's wonderful. We are reading <u>Wuthering Heights</u> now.

I have a few other things to report. One of them is that I have finally heard from my relation in Scotland. Her letter was open, though I would not go so far as to say it was warm. I've written her back. The principal of Broadneck High School reached out to me to ask if I would speak on a political science panel they are hosting in conjunction with other local high schools, and that would be in the spring. I said I probably would not, but I am considering it. Mick Watts: I did enjoy the week we spent together in Texas. While I was there he suggested a swap and he come to Annapolis to stay with me, so I'm mulling that over, but the fact of the matter is that Mick is really rather a lot. I've lived a quiet life for so long I've gotten out of practice with the way people can be, I own, but my goodness he's loud and with some massive opinions. I will say, I fully expected him to be homophobic, but when I mentioned you and Stewart, he didn't bat an eye. Goes to show, again, people can surprise you.

Warmest regards from your
loving sister,

Sybil

Sybil Van Antwerp
17 Farney Rd.
Arnold, MD 21012

21 October 2017

To Ms. Van Antwerp,

I couldn't see how you knew it was me writing when I never left
my information. I thought about it for a long time, it drove me
crazy, and then I see it's simple. You remembered. You expected
hearing from me. That surprised me really.

I have letters you sent my father, Enzo Martinelli, when he
was in prison after sentencing in 1981 by Judge Guy Donnelly in
Frederick Maryland. I found the letters years ago in my early
twenties pressed in back of a drawer in a bureau and I could not
understand, who was this woman writing to him in prison, and
did he write back? When I read the obituary for Judge Donnelly
in 2012 your name was there and I was dazed because I remembered you. You know some memories you have you wonder was
it a dream? I googled you and saw your face and the horrible
thing I wondered was maybe a memory of a bad dream, this
~~turned~~ cleared up. My mother was dragging my brother and me
on the bus down to the courthouse when she knew the judge ~~is~~
would be out—she told us this. Her name is Florencia. She said
he is at his lunchtime. How did she know that? It was a hot, sunny
day. I remember the long desk and a painting of a carnivale behind you. I was embarrassed with my mother crying. I had not
seen this before then and I didn't see her cry again for many years
later. We were learning English. My mother had a difficult time. It
embarrassed me she tripped over her words mixing Italian and
English, begging you and crying. She admitted my father ~~made a
wrongdoing~~ had done wrong! I was proud of the bread truck he
drove Pepperidge Farm Bread written along the side and his
clothes always smelled like yeast. He went out again after we

went to bed—my brother and me shared a small bed in the corner of our apartment with roaches and mice, and he filled the bread truck with other things for men who paid more money for his service. Of course it was against his contract, of course some things he put in the truck were against the law. My mother knew this—she is keen, she admitted this wrong, and she begged you. We had nothing–my parents coming from Italy with nothing, and my father ~~wanted~~ was ambitious. He tried to make a life for us, pay for school uniforms and tutors, to take us to college, wear fine clothes, go to a good school, these things. My father was full of dreams. What he did to use the truck was not good, but there was no harm to anyone and those things he delivered they would be delivered with him or someone else if it was not him, this is what my mother was pleading. My father was not ~~choosing the~~ the big man. She told you if my father went to prison our family would not survive.

Your eyes were cold and dead. Cruel. But I saw a photograph of children on your desk. I did not understand—were you a mother? I thought you were an evil witch. I remember. But maybe I see now you remember too, and that surprised me. You said for me say what I needed to say. For my life I have hated you. You grew into an enormous thing in my mind. It surprised me driving to your home. It is a pretty house and you look out to the water. It is not very large but must be expensive. I know about real estate. I saw you in the window sitting at a desk. I was watching you for a long time. How tiny you are, and you had a mailbox in the shape of a fish and a wreath on the door, these nice things. I hated you for such a long time, but you were just a small old woman and I was lost. I didn't know what to do so I cut the flowers. This didn't help.

Dezi Martinelli

Sybil Van Antwerp
17 Farney Road
Arnold, MD 21012
USA

22 October 2017

Dear Sybil,

Thank you for sending along the paperwork regarding our DNA match. I hope you won't mind, but I went and called up to my friend who is a geneticist in London and told him the whole story. I sent the paperwork to him, and he gave it a good looking over, and then I had some chats with my brothers. I suppose there's not a way to be entirely sure about the testing, but the friend of mine said the labs used by Kindred are aboveboard, as they say, and there isn't really any reason to think the report wouldn't be accurate. All of that was rather my doing a bit of stalling, and between it there is work and life. Declan, the pub-owning brother I believe I mentioned, is the keeper of the family history. He keeps the boxes of photos and paperwork, so of course when we received your letters it was to the boxes and looking through. Dec is a skeptic as well as possessive, so his first response to the whole thing was unenthusiastic. The fact is I knew Mum had a daughter before I was born, but Dec thought she'd delivered stillborn. Mum always told me the baby had died in the first few days, and I'd not had any reason to second-guess a thing like that, but it was something else you said in your first letter, which was that your DNA showed Native American parentage. My father was half Crow. It seemed too odd a coincidence to ignore.

There is an old photograph we found in the mix of my mother and father (my father's name was Charlie Thorne and it was his mother who was Crow; his father was of Spanish descent from the state of Oregon) and in it my mother is pregnant. I would have assumed it was myself in utero, but Dec and I sat with the photos for some time and there are some indicators the photo is from an earlier time, some letters (Mum was always writing and receiving letters) that indicate pregnancy at an earlier time, so I suppose, well, I suppose it might be you she's got inside. This is a very long way of going round and round to say that if what you are suggesting by reaching out to me is that we are, as strange as it is to write, sisters, then I think you must be (unless I've missed something obvious and you're quite a savvy crook) correct.

After sitting with this information these months I wish I had some way of knowing more for you. After I was born my father abandoned us. He had lived a hard going life on the drink, always gambling, and he only had one leg because of something that had happened to him in his teenage years and it'd been removed. He was meaner than a provoked snake is what I was always told, but I have no memories of him. Anyway, my mother—I suppose, it's still hard to imagine, <u>our</u> mother, <u>our</u> father—left America to return to Scotland, where she was born. Gleason is her surname, and she gave it to me rather than Thorne. She married a Welshman here in Scotland and together they had Declan, John, and Douglas. He stood in as a father for me and I was nary the wiser until when I went to university and Mum told me the truth, and that did explain a great deal because I have very dark features and the rest of them are freckled and fair haired. Mum died in 1998 with lung cancer (she was a smoker), and I wouldn't say she told me very much about her life outside Scotland, between her early teenage years to her late twenties. When I did a few months with the Kindred website it was because I had an itch to find some information on my father, and I dug up his obituary from out somewhere in Montana and it was something brief and impersonal from a local paper, but here is what I learned. His name was Charles Broderick Thorne, eldest of two children to David and Mildred Thorne, born 1 September 1917 in Portland, Oregon. He died in a strange way, and that was being stampeded by a herd of cattle. I read that and it's stuck in my mind these years. Terribly gruesome. I don't think if Mum ever had another point of contact with him after we'd left for Scotland.

One doesn't know how to bring a letter of this sort to a close. There isn't a template for such a thing. I've sat here for quite some time, and I don't know what else to say other than you get to be seventy-four and you think it'll be a nice easy coast to the end, and then you find out all along you had a sister living in Washington, DC. I guess I would like to know about you. What has come to pass in your life?

Enclosed is the photo I mentioned of Mum pregnant with you. Have I said—would you know, I guess you wouldn't know—her name was Louisa. I have also enclosed a photo of myself and Dec, Douggie, and John from Christmas a year or two ago. I very much look forward to your reply,

Hattie

Sybil Van Antwerp
17 Farney Rd.
Arnold, MD 21012
USA

November 15, 2017

Syb,

Stewart cheated and I'm coming back. I booked a flight to Dulles for December 3 because I'm speaking at a salon on the second. Can you pick me up? I land in the early evening. What are the Christmas plans? If I'm still there then, and you have arranged for the upstairs to be occupied by Fiona, I can vacate. Spoke to Suzanne and Bob this morning and they have their guesthouse and they said I'm welcome to it. I despise Los Angeles, but that dry, consistent climate suits me and they're really more toward the hills than the city anyway.

I'm heartbroken. Seventeen years—SMACK—just like that, shattered. Makes me realize how Stewart was braided into everything. My work, my routines, my friendships, meals, movie watching, book reading, walking, waking up, drinking coffee. Makes you wonder what any of it was for. What it meant. Casts every good thing in an ugly green, doesn't it?

Well, my dear. I'll see you soon,

Felix

Harry Landy
Florence Moore Hall
Stanford University
436 Mayfield Ave.
Stanford, CA 94305

November 25, 2017

Dear Harry,

Happy Thanksgiving. How are you, dear? I haven't heard from you in some time, but my hope is that it means you have been busy with learning and friends out in California. Is that the reason? I do hope you are happy. Your father seems to think you are, but your father tends to be easily charmed by rosy delusions, as you and I both know. How are your studies coming? How is the building of the video game coming along? Your father told me you've got the attention of internet people in the Silicon Valley. Haven't I always said the only different thing about you is you're smarter than the rest of us idiots? I always like to see when I'm proved right.

I am writing to see if you might be willing to use your internet navigation capabilities along with your Stanford library access and do a favor for me. Would you be willing to look up one CHARLES BRODERICK THORNE. Born September 1, 1917, Portland, Oregon. Anything you could find would be helpful, any old thing. I have it on good authority the man died in a cattle stampede.

If you do find anything, Harry, please refrain from sending me an e-mail with long strings of characters in blue I'm meant to click. The last time you did that I became so lost in the internet I had to press the button on the computer itself to turn it off and then start over when I turned it back on. What would be best is if you could print anything you find (in as large a size as possible)

and mail it to me. I understand this makes things more complicated for you.

I have additional news to report. I did write to Dezi Martinelli
in September.

With love,

Ms. Van Antwerp

Ms. Van Antwerp
17 Farney Rd.
Arnold, MD
21012

December 23, 2017

Dear Ms. Van Antwerp,

I found three documents through the Stanford library databases and ejournals that mention the Charles Broderick Thorne I think you want. There was also a Charles Broadwater Thorne born in 1921 in Birmingham, Alabama, and his records have gotten mixed with your Charles Thorne, but I think I can figure out which one is which. The one you're looking for also went by Charlie. I printed the articles and enlarged the type as much as I could.

I was thinking about coming to visit you this summer. I have an internship for June and July, but I'm coming home the first week of August.

Sincerely,

Harry Landy

P.S. Dad is right. I think I am happy. I think he is very unhappy with my mom back in the hospital.

Enclosure 1

CHARLES BRODERICK THORNE
Charles Broderick Thorne

Charles B. Thorne died tragically on Monday, July 8, 1959, in Youngsport, Montana, in a cattle stampede. Charlie Thorne leaves his wife of three years, Susannah Thorne, and their two sons, Davie (5) and Joe (4), behind. Charlie Thorne was born on September 1, 1917, in Portland, Oregon, and is additionally survived by one brother, Eugene P. Thorne of Spokane, Washington. Funeral services to be held Sunday, July 13, (closed casket) at the Holy Trinity Methodist Chapel in the town of Dove, where Mrs. Thorne and the children reside. No viewing.

Enclosure 2

STAMPEDE OUTSIDE YOUNGSPORT KILLS THREE MEN
Youngsport Gazette Tuesday, July 9, 1959

Yesterday just after six in the evening a herd of cattle owned by Ulysses Fitzgerald was spooked into a stampede. It is believed that a rattlesnake under the feet of a single cow was the origin of the disorder, although Youngsport Sheriff P. B. Tacoma is investigating the possibility of foul play. The more than three hundred cattle took off south toward Star Canyon, and three hands on the south side of the canyon were killed. The men who died were Howard Valour of Quebec, Charlie Thorne of nearby town Dove, Montana, and Peter Nubbin, known locally as Skinny Pete.

The cattle were rounded up, four dead, and Fitzgerald will pay damages to the mourning families.

Enclosure 3

Manifest of Passengers Aboard the SS *Adriatic,* White Star Line, New York to Liverpool
3rd Class
Departure from New York, New York, October 30, 1943
Harland & Wolfe, Belfast

Thomas, Ian & Marie
Thomas, Mark & Sorcha
    with children, Gerard, John, Roisin and Marie
Thorne, Louisa
    with child, Henrietta (husband, Charles B. Thorne
    deceased)
Thosburn, Hermit
Tibley, Hamilton

(cont. Dec. 25, 2017, *previous pages UNSENT*)

We are having a white Christmas. I haven't seen snow on Christmas in years, and this morning I woke up to a dusting and powdered sugar is coming down outside the window as I write. It's really quite beautiful.

It was Enzo's son after all, as I knew it was. Somehow I knew it was Dezi. In some ways, I've been waiting for him all these years. I could see it in his eyes that time he came to see me, that he would be back eventually. He is angry with me, of course he is, but even all the time I was reading the lashing he sent me by mail, there was something in it I was wanting. Something in it I was glad to receive, finally.

People assume a certain high morality of judges, but judges are merely people. There were many decisions over which Guy and I agonized, and you know, you make a decision and you hope and pray it's the right one—but you're not God on high with the ability to see all things! You're human! The outcomes don't exist yet. But this case, Enzo's case, was different. This one—I knew we were wrong. Right away. I knew we were wrong before it was decided.

I look in the mirror and how can it be? I am an old woman. What has my life been, really? I'll go blind, and then? I wonder— the letters. All the letters. I wonder if all of it was a waste. Pages and pages of letters. I wonder what has it all been, really. I'll go blind, and they will be nothing to me. It will be as if they aren't there, and does that mean, in a way, they were never there? I'm not sure. Dezi said something to me. He said there are complexities of human life that cannot be boiled down to black and white. Of course! Of course.

Dear Theodore,

Thank you for the Yule cake. When I was married I used to buy Daan kitchen items—good knives, a garlic press, a Bundt pan—for Christmas, and it was a joke we had, that when we were in retirement, he could take up cooking and I could at last devote my life and attentions to reading and correspondence and we would both live out our days in euphoria. Of course, Daan didn't care a thing for being in the kitchen, and as it turns out I will not have much more time for reading or correspondence. You know I have trouble with my eyes, but I have not told you that I have a condition that is greedily circling, ready to render me blind. I have known about it for some time. As it is now, lately when I wake up it takes such a long time before my eyes can come into focus, and there is the odd day when I can't see out of one or both eyes at all.

I did want to address another matter directly, and that is I have the sense your manner toward me grew cold when I mentioned the upcoming visit from Mick Watts. I'll pop the head off the dandelion stem right here in no uncertain terms. At seventy-eight years old I have no intention of ever remarrying and I assure you I will conduct my life as I see fit, and if that means I pass some of my days with one man and other days with someone else, that is my choice to make. If it troubles you, then I suggest you reverse and go find somewhere else to park yourself. Mick Watts is a friend of mine, and our lives share a substantial quantity of overlap. Mick is funny and clever, and we have a good time together. I want nothing to do with it if you continue to conduct yourself in a snit.

If we see eye to eye on that, there is something I would like to show you pertaining to the massacre of my flowerbeds two springs ago. I find myself in need of assistance. We can discuss the matters of Mick and my flowerbeds on Monday when I come for cards and scotch. I'll be glad to close the door on 2017. It has been a difficult year for me, but even still one must, for respect of auld lang syne, salute each annum with respect and ownership,

Sybil

Dezi Martinelli
138 South Carrington St.
Hasbrouck Heights, NJ 07604

January 8, 2018

Dear Dezi,

I received your letter of October 21, 2017. I can see only one way to begin, and that is to tell you, yes, I do remember you and your brother, Aldo, very well. I remember the day your mother brought you to Judge Donnelly's chambers, and I remember the circumstances of the case. In fact, all of this has stayed very vivid in my memory for many years, and as troubling as it was to read your furious letter, it was also something of a relief. It seems age is softening me.

I am going blind. I am not telling you this as a plea for sympathy. When I was told by my eye doctor seven or eight years ago it was as if suddenly I was waking up from a long dream, a dream that had been my entire life, and now here was the real life and a timer had been set. When my eyes go, that will be the end of me, I thought, and the notion of the end of my life, though it feels trite to say, made me reminisce and consider the past in ways I had not done. You should know that among other things, there you were. You, your mother, your brother, and your father, Enzo.

About four weeks before your father's case came before Judge Donnelly (and, therefore, me) my son died. He was eight years old. He was the middle of my three children. If you have suffered the death of a child, you have my complete sympathy and you do not require me to go on. If you have not, then suffice it to say there is no greater pain. Imagine the most severe pain, multiply it by a thousand. Ten thousand. Then you will have some inkling. Gilbert died, and two weeks later I returned to work and the matter of your father's hearing. In your letter you said my eyes were cold and dead and cruel when you met me, and you are correct. I was cold, dead, and cruel. Was I a mother? I was asking myself the same. I was an evil witch, yes. If you had said these things to me that day, I would have said yes. I would have relished it.

Here is the whole truth, and this is my confession: when your mother came into my office with her two perfect, healthy sons begging for Judge Donnelly to have mercy on your father, I was cold and cruel. I hated her because she had you. Your big, curious eyes. How like Gilbert you seemed to me. The cowlick at the back of your head. Your brother with his socks sagging down at his ankles. She introduced you—"my sons Dezi and Aldo." It was as if she'd stabbed me with a knife. You were tall and thin, and I could see you were paying attention. She begged for mercy, and I thought, I admit it, my thought was if I could not have my family back, then why should she? There had been no mercy shown to me; why should anyone receive mercy? My misery made me cruel. When Donnelly returned from lunch he said the secretary at the courthouse said I'd met with the defendant's wife. He came to me, wondering why your mother had come, but I waved him off. I did not plead on her behalf, as I should have, as I, a mother, should have. I knew I had his ear, and I did not speak up for your mother. When Donnelly delivered your father's sentence, the harsh sentence I knew he would deliver, I was silent, I relished my silence in that moment, and for this I am sorry.

After the sentencing, though, I was haunted. Your father's testimony, your visit, it all bothered me. I was outside my mind during that time, unable to sleep, deranged with grief, and I became fixated on your family in a way, some parallel guilt, I guess. After a while I wrote to your father in prison, just a short thing with a few dollars. I didn't confide in him, really, just a little note to say I hoped he was getting on OK, but he wrote back. His response was a beautiful letter, honest. He was so young, not thirty, but gentle. He said he wasn't angry with me, he was so gracious. So wise. It moved me. We exchanged a handful of letters, the letters you have seen, and I always included a few dollars he could use at the commissary, but his letters rather always surprised me. Even though I kept myself at a distance, he told me little things about his life in Bergamo, and how he had fallen in love with your mother when he was just a boy, his happiness with having had sons. He told me that he'd only wanted to make something for you and your brother. He talked about the dream of buying a house with a garden for vegetables for your mother, Florencia. He said when he got out of prison he planned to go to you all in Italy and bring you back.

The last time I wrote him it was returned to me because he'd been released. I'd never really apologized to him for my part in the outcome of his life, though I guess he knew I was sorry. Where is your father now? I think I'd like to write to him again, to apologize.

With respect,

Sybil Van Antwerp

Hattie Gleason
Bodney Cottage
Fassfern
Fort William PH33 7NP
Scotland

February 2, 2018

Dear Hattie,

Thank you for your letter, and for the photos you sent. Though I have spent what must amount by now to hours staring at the one of your pregnant mother and father, and though I agree it seems we are very likely family, I cannot seem to find a way for the information to take up residence in my body. The strangest thing is to see the resemblance I share with you, and with the man in the photo with the pregnant woman, my father. What is more, that full, beautiful strawberry-blond hair she had is precisely identical to my daughter's hair, and I had wondered where those genes came from. Remarkable. My brother (by adoption) was here over the holidays and I told him about all of this. I showed him the photos and with one look he was absolutely certain your family is mine. I am enclosing a photograph of myself. The similarity of our faces is remarkable.

I am finding I have nowhere to put all of this. I'm sorry, but do you know what I mean? It's like I've come home from the grocery store overburdened with bags, but the cupboards, the refrigerator, the pantry, the countertop are all already full. A mother and father? But I had a mother and father. Siblings? I have a sibling. It feels a betrayal to even acknowledge you exist! No vacancy. No room at the inn. We're all full up, and yet the thing I always thought was so small now seems as enormous as a galaxy, this thing I have felt my whole life, and that is, a sense of something missing, this curiosity of why my mother let me go. I haven't the tools for it though. How to open myself up, let the flood wash over and through.

My life was simple enough. My parents who adopted me were wonderful. My mother had a cancer of the cervix when she was only twenty-four, so she had everything removed, and that meant she was unable to have children. They adopted me, and then my brother from Sisters in Ireland, County Clare, and raised us beautifully, put us through private school and college. The cancer ended up coming back to kill her via the bloodstream when I was eighteen. My dad was a banker and he did very well. My parents were typical American middle-class conservatives, and my father remarried quickly. Nobody wants a stepmother, but mine was fine and I was already out of the house. I will say, when it turned out Felix was gay (he came right out with it before it was an acceptable thing to do, age seventeen), they didn't miss a beat, my father and his second wife, so in that she earned my respect. You don't hear that story often, do you? I guess, compared to your life, and your mother's, I should be grateful for the ease of my own. I married and we had three children. One died young, so I'm down to two, and I've made a mess of it. My daughter barely speaks to me. Apparently she's had miscarriages and didn't tell me. I have grandchildren now, too. My husband and I divorced, and he has passed away from cancer. Cancer cancer cancer.

I had a career in law. I was a clerk to a judge. Judge Guy Donnelly. I was rather like a cross between his wife and his conscience and his silent counselor. I guess this is the most interesting thing about me, though I hope you don't think I go around parading this thing like some kind of badge of honor (I do not). It was a very large part of my life, for better or for worse. My career was wonderful for me, but hard on my family, and this is a roundabout way of explaining why my husband and I split up. Well, it's part of the reasoning.

In any case, my life has recently taken a surprising turn. Last week I hosted a man at my house. He wants to marry me. Oh, it isn't that he's produced a ring and got down on his knee, but from the second dinner he's said we should marry. Can you believe such a thing? Anyway, I don't have any interest in being married at this point, and it's a bit of a complexity because I have this other friend, a man who's a neighbor, and that complicates things—I'm going on and on, and you don't even know me.

Perhaps you might be willing to tell me a little bit more about yourself. I think I might also like to know just a little bit more about your mother. Additionally, a friend of mine who is an expert in internet researching found three documents pertaining to Charlie Thorne, and I've enclosed copies of them here, for your interest. It appears we share two additional half-brothers by the names of Davie and Joe.

Warm regards,

Sybil

Sybil Van Antwerp
17 Farney Road
Arnold, MD 21012

April 9, 2018

Dear Sybil,

It was so nice to get your letter, and thank you for the book of poetry. I was somewhat familiar with Eavan Boland, but had not read much. The opening poem, "Quarantine," is stunning.

I did notice the change in your penmanship and I am sorry to hear your eyesight has taken a downturn. It's a fear I had for many years, losing my sight. It would be a significant loss. However, it's wonderful your neighbor installed the magnifying device for you at your desk. The contraption sounds cumbersome but worthwhile. He sounds like a good person to have next door. You asked if I still write. I do, only less.

Between Mick's interest in marrying you and this fascinating discovery of a sister in Scotland, your life has become very exciting. What will you do about the Texas man? I look forward to hearing how it unfolds. With love—

Joan

Sybil Van Antwerp
17 Farney Rd.
Arnold, MD 21012

29 April 2018

Dear Ms. Van Antwerp,

I read your letter. It was very full. I am surprised to be saying this, but I am sorry your son Gilbert died. My oldest daughter is with the angels. She left us the day after she was born, that was in 1992.

In spring last year 2015 my son took an overdose of heroin. The good rehab programs are so expensive. We took another mortgage on our house. He lives, but he is not the same, and we are always in worry. I think I can understand your sadness.

One thing, I wasn't clear. My father is dead. He died when I was fifteen years old. This occurred in a terrible way. He got out of jail and borrowed money to come to Italy. By then he was like a dog in a junkyard. He was drinking and ill from it. He wanted my mother to come back to America and they would try again, but she was angry and would not have him. Life was very hard on her, and she was a black sheep because of my father's crime. She is the second daughter in a family with four sisters, and my grandfather was not a rich man. He was of the mind she married a fool. Everyone knew she had gone away to America, and come back without my father. Everyone knew everything somehow. We were living with my nonna on the edge of Bergamo. My grandfather had died. My father arrived on the porch. My mother did not let him in the house because he was ragged and drunk. On this same night he went to a bar and after some hours they said he went out and he was hit by a car in the street. He died five days later in the hospital there. My papa was a good man, but this is the outcome. I think this is the reason I have been so angry.

My mother lives in Italy still, but I came to America when

I was nineteen. I have an Italian sandwich and meats shop in Hoboken called Nelli's, which you may have heard if you have been in the area. The oil and vinegar blend I use is selling in most grocery stores in the Northeast and out west as far as Ohio.

Best regards,

Dezi Martinelli

TO: sybilvanantwerp@aol.com

FROM: MansourBas850@hotmail.com

DATE: May 5, 2018 01:14 AM

SUBJECT: A job for me

Dear Ms. Van Antwerp,

How are you doing? How are your eyes holding up? Are you maintaining correspondence with your biological sister?

Last time we emailed it was early in the year, and I am sorry for the long stretch. We have had a great deal of trouble the last months. Zoha had a seizure in February while she was at school. I was working and Kalee was at a house where she takes care of an elderly man, and unable to leave because I had the car. I left the office where I am working now and rushed to the hospital in San Francisco and she was sedated and intubated. She had fallen and knocked her head, so she had part of her beautiful hair shaved and a terrible sutured incision.

The reason I took the job I was in is because of the health insurance, which is not much, but is better than none at all. Health care in the US is very complex (at Kindred, the insurance was excellent). Zoha was in the hospital for three weeks while they were testing her to understand the origin of the seizure and we came away without the answer, but the doctors are saying it may happen again at any time and there is no way of knowing when or what causes it, plus the very expensive hospital charges.

During this time, Emir was having problems in school. He was having poor grades on tests and having his teachers calling to tell us and he has a few boys who are his friends, but they are troublesome and they lit a small tree in a park on fire one evening when Kalee and I were still at work. He was picked up by the police. The officer was kind and did not log the incident, but of course it was terrible. He cannot do these things. It is very shameful to himself, and to his mother and me, and to other Syrian families we know here. I whipped him and took away his social privileges for three months (this is difficult to enforce when we are at work, however). We brought the children here to shield them from the life we left, to give them this good life in America. I don't want them to know what we left behind because it is terrible. I am always trying to protect them, every decision is striving to protect them, and yet somehow we are doing things wrong.

This is all very bad news, and yet I have something hopeful to share with you. Dale Woodson interviewed me for the second time, this time with three of his colleagues, and I think he will offer me a job. It felt very good talking to them about the things I know. I remember when you said in an email that when you find a place for yourself in the world, it feels like music, and I thought of that, sitting over the table with Dale Woodson and talking about highway infrastructure. I guess I am a very boring sort of person, but to me highway infra-structure is a symphony.

This email is to tell you thank you, Ms. Van Antwerp, for setting a new course for my life.

With most sincere appreciation and respect,
Basam Mansour

Felix Stone
℅ Suzanne and Bob Archer
104 Merry Acres Pl.
Verdugo Hills, CA 91042

May 14, 2018

Dearest Felix,

How are you getting on in Los Angeles? How is your work? Are you making points of contact out there? Now that you've been in place for nearly five months I have wondered if you will stay. Have you spoken to Stewart, dear? Does he continue to seek you out? Would it not be worth even considering the possibility of at least hearing what the man has to say? Although I miss you and wish you would move closer to me rather than farther away, France is so obviously where you belong.

There have been no additional letters from Hattie, though it's been her turn for some time. I really can't blame her, though, can I? It's a strange situation we're in. I believe she works a great deal, too, and I'm sure there is an outside notion that this is all still somehow untoward.

While I wait to hear from her I find myself reading everything I can get my hands on regarding Scotland, as well as the Crow tribe of Indians (scratch that, we're meant to say Native Americans now). There was a lecture at St. John's College, as a matter of fact, regarding the displacement of native tribes in the Northwest and I attended with Theodore Lübeck. I do enjoy his company, but moreover I was needing a driver. My eyes are giving me some trouble, Felix, so I thought with it being evening it was better not to drive down. And the parking in Annapolis can be a challenge, all the teens wandering into the streets without paying attention.

Additionally (I've saved the worst for last) over here on my side of the nation there is a big, fat situation. Mick Watts was in DC again, and this time he didn't make excuses. He flew across just to take me to dinner in Baltimore, and it was lovely, and at the end of dinner there was a ring and Mick asked me to marry him formally. As I have previously told you, he has mentioned wanting to marry me several times, but rather in an off the cuff manner and I have shoved off the notion each time, but this was a different thing, with him in a suit, the ring, the lights on the harbor all glittering out the window, the steak and the white tablecloth and the nice bottle of cabernet. He was asking seriously. He wants me to move to Texas with him.

I'm certain you're wondering what I said, and I'll tell you. I told him I would have to think it over. It isn't as if I'm in my twenties and just beginning a life, making those choices that become the pavers of a path which you walk. I've made my path. It's difficult to imagine whipping the entire thing around and starting something new. I'm not sure I have the energy for it, and yet it's such good fun with Mick, and it is a comfort, isn't it, imagining someone else around a house. Someone to rather, well, I suppose, take care of me. With Mick I laugh such a great deal. It is the version of myself I was when I was working. Whip-smart, clever, well able for the banter and the debating politics.

Now, of course I always welcome your thoughts on every matter, but in this case, I beg you to tread thoughtfully because I fear I'm so perplexed by the matter that anything you say might make tracks I'd be unable to erase.

I do look forward to hearing from you, and of course I welcome you to come spend a bit of time on the East Coast if you please. I haven't been writing many letters the past few months. I come to the desk and have no energy for the task. But you're not to worry. I decided I would sit on the panel for the high school career festival. That's next week.

That is more than enough out of me, and I am sending my very warmest regards,

Your loving sister,

Sybil

Ms. Van Antwerp
17 Farney Road
Arnold, MD 21012

July 31, 2018

Dear Ms. Van Antwerp,

Thank you for the book you sent. I had not read John McGahern, and in fact I have not read much Irish literature aside from the standards (Joyce, Yeats, Beckett). After reading <u>Amongst Women</u>, I went and read <u>That They May Face the Rising Sun</u>, which I liked very much, and then I felt the desire to remain in Ireland, so I picked up <u>The Stories of William Trevor</u> and I'm going slowly, reading one story per week so it lasts.

I'm enclosing the course schedule for the fall term. Please feel free to choose any class(es) you like. Would you consider auditing my poetry seminar? Just the once? There is a course that follows the time slot that is Modern American Literature, and it's a professor we got from UCLA this fall. His syllabus includes Roth. Do you like Roth? People say you either love or hate Roth, and I've found that to be true. I won't tell you which side I'm on yet. Anyway, you could come on Wednesdays and sit for poetry from 11 to 1, break for lunch, then sit for Modern American from 1:45 to 4.

You asked about my summer holiday. Most of June was crap, spent planning for the semester and putting out fires. My mother-in-law passed away and our most recent round of IVF failed, but my husband and I did travel a bit after the memorial in early July. We went to Lisbon, where we stayed for two luxurious weeks, then we went to Croatia and Greece. I live to travel. I wrote a great deal of poetry, which was wonderful, reacquainting me with myself. Do you enjoy travel?

And yes, I will go into the year as you said: boldly, unapologetically, head up and not taking bullshit from anyone with a penis. You seem a worthy person to offer such advice.

Fondly,

Melissa Genet

University of Maryland,
College Park
College Park, MD

TO: Roy@coastaleyepartners.com
FROM: sybilvanantwerp@aol.com
DATE: Aug 19, 2018 7:33PM
SUBJECT: Trouble seeing

Dear Dr. Jameson,

It's in the last week or so I am suddenly finding it much more difficult
to see.

Warm regards,
Sybil Van Antwerp

TO: sybilvanantwerp@aol.com
FROM: Roy@coastaleyepartners.com
DATE: Aug 20, 2018 3:48PM
SUBJECT: RE: Trouble seeing

Dear Sybil,

I'm glad you reached out. I'd like to put you on the schedule for next
week. I'll have my assistant give you a call to find a time. Do you
have someone who could bring you?

Roy

TO: Roy@coastaleyepartners.com
FROM: sybilvanantwerp@aol.com
DATE: Aug 21, 2018 7:03AM
SUBJECT: RE: Re: Trouble seeing

Dear Dr. Jameson,

Please do have your assistant call me rather than sending an appointment through e-mail. My neighbor will be happy to drive me to the appointment, and many thanks.

Sybil

Dear Sybil,

I got your note (I was at the Annapolis Mall cinema) and I am happy to drive you to your appointment on September 4 at 9:40 in the morning. I have been somewhat worried about you. I don't mind if you aren't up for visiting, but I don't see you in the garden or out walking. I have not seen the cars of visitors at your house. It would be nice if we could go out to lunch following your appointment. You haven't told me what came to pass with the son of Enzo.

You don't need to thank me for showing you how to enlarge the type on your screen. It was my daughter who showed me. And you're most welcome for the magnifying scheme.

Speaking of my daughter, I've decided I will go on the trip to Germany. It would be foolish to wait. She wants to see the place her mother and I are from, and to see the graves of my ancestors. It seems to mean something to her, so I'll be going. Gone a month, leaving in a few weeks, but the fall is keeping hot and I wonder if you would be willing to water the roses. I'll be happy to provide the watering schedule. I'll have the post office hold the mail.

You haven't mentioned if you have yet accepted Mick's proposal. I'm happy for you. You seem very happy with him.

Your friend,

Theodore

Fiona Van Antwerp-Beaumont
2 Hamilton Terrace
London SE 28 8JF
United Kingdom

September 17, 2018

Dear Fiona,

It's a few days since our disastrous phone call. I've been reflecting on the things you said and replaying our harsh words. I was rather immobilized at the time, and I am certain I said things I didn't mean. Perhaps I ought to call you, but I am better with the pen and the paper (even though, as you now know, I won't be able to write much longer with the oncoming blindness), and today my vision is a bit less murky. It is difficult to know where to begin, although I do know what needs to be said.

You said I am critical of the way you live your life, and that you (and Walt, the children) are trying to do it the opposite of the way I did it. This was very painful to hear. When you brought up that I disapprove of your career path, I was so surprised. Even though I had presumed you would go into medicine, as you had talked about for years leading up to the conclusion of your undergraduate studies, and it took me some time to adjust to your pivot toward architecture, I am unashamedly proud of the career you have built. More painful, when I raised the subject of your miscarriages, and finding out about it from Aunt Rosalie, you said that you hadn't told me about it because you don't how to confide in me, that I am very distant. My response to you was that you have never seemed to need me, and you said that I taught you not to need me. Well, perhaps you can imagine how it would feel to hear these things from Frannie one day. Terrible.

My instinct is to fight, and initially I found myself rather compiling a case, disputing your accusations, thinking of all the proof I have that you're wrong. And yet I waited. I continued to sit with it. Surprising even myself, I've let the tide go out with my self-defense, but I do want to tell you a story about me.

When I was a child your grandparents sat me down to explain that I was adopted. I was in first grade. Your Pop had come home from work and we sat down in the formal living room, which was unusual, and they explained it to me, and then they took me for an ice cream sundae in lieu of supper to smooth it all over. I was troubled by it. Of course I was, but I was something of a weird bird as a child (serious, grave, without friends, often ignored by other children) and tended toward fixating on things. I became fixated on this. It has always been my nature to see things in black and white, as you well know. I like rules. I relish living in a world that runs on laws and systems that are quite clear and declared. I think being adopted made me feel, as a child, that I did not fit inside the system. I didn't tell a soul.

My parents, knowing how it plagued me, a few years later gave me a letter that my birth mother had written before handing me over and I became obsessed with this piece of paper in a light pink envelope. I kept it in a small wooden box under my bed. For months I read it every night before sleep. I studied her script. I tried to read between the lines, between the letters, to see if I could find something maybe I'd missed. It was agonizing. I wanted my birth mother desperately, though I kept it to myself. Her name was Louisa, which I have only come to know through the Kindred membership your brother gave me for Christmas all those years back. I am enclosing the letter. Please keep it.

I began writing letters because my birth mother (as a child I thought of her as my 'real' mother) had, apparently, written letters. I clung to this and did actually find, through correspondence, inexplicable relief. I could write to anyone. I could take the time to think through what I wanted to say, practice, rewrite, and get it exactly how I wanted it. It was so much easier for me to write than it was to have a conversation, even. I was insecure, painfully so. I felt so strange. On the phone the other night you mentioned this, that you wondered if maybe I could only have meaningful relationships through letters, and I have been thinking about that. When I was young, by writing letters I found a framework that made living easier, and that has never changed. However, I do wonder if by conducting the most intimate relationships of my life in correspondence, I have kept, since I was a child, a distance between myself and others. I think it's true the letters have insulated me, have been a force field, just as practicing law insulated me from dealing with humanity directly, and I wouldn't change any of it, but I find myself, at this old age, wanting closeness. I want <u>closeness</u>. Something I have not had other than when I met Dad.

Meeting your dear dad was the great surprise of my life because I'd never imagined I would have THAT. I thought I would need someone to find me bearable, but he thought I was wonderful! And I thought him even better. He never made me feel strange. He gave me a family—I'd outwitted the fate I'd assumed for myself. He taught me how to open myself to others. I had never done that. It was healing for me. He thought I was wonderful, and I'll always love him for that.

When you were born I was terrified. With the two boys I felt I was in a position I could manage—they seemed like foreign objects—but then you came out, a girl. I was afraid to have a girl because what if I couldn't understand you? I'd never found a way to fit into the world, not really, and what if I didn't know how to be a mother to you? I was afraid, and that's the whole thing. I was afraid all the time of losing something or ruining something, and then I did.

When Gilbert died you were only four. His death—toppled me. I ~~couldn't~~ had worked to do everything correctly, follow the rules, wedge myself into the world, but it wasn't enough. Fiona, do you know what it feels like when your worst fear, your very worst fear, comes to pass? When the imagined terror comes true? I hope you never do. I couldn't make any sense of it. The life I had built was not strong enough; the laws of nature were too unwieldy for me to surmount. ~~It was the~~ I could not bear it, and that steeling, locking the agony in, and pushing you away because what if I lost you, too? What if I lost Bruce? I pulled back from you. If I didn't feel as much to begin with, then it wouldn't come as hard when, not if, but WHEN my fears came to pass again. I suppose I've never recovered. I do not know how to recover.

Fiona, I am putting words to something I have not put words to ever in my life. The being adopted, Gilbert's dying, the end of my marriage, I always felt—all wrong. Like I was a fraud, acting, pretending I was a daughter, a wife, a mother. I wanted to be those things, and I suppose I was, but I rather never believed it, and then so many things went wrong. Your brother's death shattered me and I've never been put back to right. It seems Dad was able to continue in love, where I was unable. Grief (the biggest grief in the world) is like—What? What is it that happens to a person? I've always felt it is like a scream living inside me. It's gotten a bit softer over time, but it's never gone. I walk around the house or dig in the garden or wander the grocery store or sit at my desk and there's a screaming inside my head like an air horn that warns of war.

When I look back at my life as a mother I have a pervasive sense of failure, and yet look at you. Your life is full and good, and so is your brother's. Fiona, I am sorry I've kept you at an arm's length, teaching you not to need me. I am sorry I was bitter that you visited Rosalie and punished you for it. I'm sorry I didn't tell you I am going blind. I'm sorry I didn't do better. I know you think of me as your mother only, but please remember, inside I am also just a girl.

I have been in touch lately with the child of a man Guy and I sentenced to prison years ago. It was an error of judgment we made, and the outcome was devastating for this family. I've only found out recently that the man is dead. He's been dead for decades. All of this has occupied my focus the past few months. You must think I am outside my mind. I am grieved, and exhausted. This letter has grown into a thick tangle of complicated thoughts, taken me hours of squinting, but I hope it makes some sense to you.

Took a break and walked outside, had a chat with the neighbor Mr. Lübeck. I'll be needing to get back to Mr. Watts with my answer about marriage soon. I can't put him off forever. You haven't told me what you think. What do you think?

I love you,

Mom

Postscript: I have yet to tell your brother or your uncle Felix about the eye condition, but I'll go ahead and do that. Please let me be the one to do that. I'll make sure it's soon.

Rosalie Van Antwerp
33 Orange Lane
Goshen, CT 06756

Dear Rosalie,

I am writing to put an end to the long silence. I'm calling this week my parade of apologies, so you can exhale and read on with smug confidence (not that you will; you're not like me).

Before I get to that, though, I wanted to ask you—in a letter quite a while back you mentioned putting Lars in a home. Greenmont Village. Have you done so over the course of my distance? I am sick over the thought that you may have done during these many weeks we haven't spoken. The conflict you feel, or felt, is awful awful. You said it feels like giving up, but it is not. You are not aspiring to a dream; you are trying to survive. You are trying to outwit the challenges that have tried their damnedest to topple you. I wanted to say that to you, first and foremost.

Things boiled over with Fiona, as they were always destined to, I see now, in hindsight. It's true what they say about hindsight. We were talking on the phone, it was about a week ago now, and I had mentioned not seeing her in some time, and she positively exploded, went into a diatribe of her grievances against me like the projectile innards of a dirty bomb. I retaliated with the intel I've harbored of her visit to you, and that backfired because she said she already knew I knew. It was terrible, but in my head, as she unleashed, was the letter you sent last summer and for the first time since reading it I felt not hurt by you, but loved. Under direct fire from Fiona, I sat in the kitchen and wished beyond comprehension that you were sitting there across from me, hearing the conversation, urging me forward. Oh, I said some terrible things right back, in the heat of that moment, but after the phone call I went into hibernation for a few days to have a long sit and think. I reread your letter and this whole thing slowly turned over, like a fat whale on a beach, FLOP, and then I had clarity. I wrote to Fiona. Obviously it was a letter to apologize, but I also flayed myself open like a caught fish. I mailed the letter yesterday, and now I'm fretting.

All right, now here it is, Rosalie, I might as well get on with it, the reason I'm writing today. I AM SORRY. I was angry with you unjustly. Please forgive me. I lost months—not months, a year or more! God save me—of confiding in you because of my blindness, and I wasn't present for you in a difficult time, and everything you said to me regarding Fiona was a blunt kindness, but I let my stubbornness override my allegiance to you. I can't take it back, but I want to say that I see my error—I am seeing so clearly! Isn't it ironic?—and I am so very, very sorry, Rosalie. Please take me back. Please write to me and tell me everything. How you are, and Paul, and Lars. You are an unassailable and miraculous creature, Rosalie. I hope you'll take me back. I can't do it without you.

All right, now that's done, thank God.

Other things have happened of which I would like you to be aware. Mick Watts proposed formally and wants to sweep me away to Texas. Stewart cheated on Felix, so they broke up and Felix is in Los Angeles and doing poorly. Things came to a head with the dean of English at UMDCP, the result of which is that we became friends and I am taking a poetry course. I will also need to talk to you on the phone to tell you about another very strange, complex, horrible thing that has happened over the course of the past few years related to a case Guy heard in the seventies. Lastly, I have heard nothing from Hattie Gleason in some time. That's all.

Write me,

Sybil

Postscript: I am reading with greater difficulty now. Trying to get through <u>Pride and Prejudice</u> one more time. Sometimes I can see enough to write; for instance, today it's rather clear, and sometimes it's nearly impossible. I thought when I started to lose my sight in this way, when it actually began to slip away, I would cling to it with all my might, but that isn't the way I feel now. Now that it's become such a strain, I almost find myself ready to let it go. Not totally, and you know I might go back on that tomorrow, but today that is how I feel.

TO: sybilvanantwerp@aol.com
FROM:stewartpbates@gmail.com
DATE: Oct 2, 2018 08:08 PM
SUBJECT: Felix

Hi Sybil,

I hope you're doing well, enjoying your grandkids. Did you get my letter? I assume you're angry with me, and you'd have a right to be, but you don't know the whole story. Felix himself doesn't know the whole story, but he is still unwilling to take my calls or texts, or open my emails. I would get on a plane, but I don't even know where he's staying. I imagine you think that by standing between the two of us you are protecting your brother, but it's not the case. Felix and I need to talk. I'm almost certain that if we could just talk, I could apologize and explain, we could get the train back on the tracks.

This is what happened. I got to know a Frenchman too well. It was a mistake. Felix and I had been having some troubles. Felix was writing a long essay and it wasn't going well. He had placement for it, and then the funding for the anthology fell through around the time he was finally breaking through his mental block, and he was disappointed. As you know, when the work is going well he is happy, and when it's not, he becomes far-off, selfish, and sullen. It'd been months (or longer) of the latter and I was tired of it. We fought, he brought up marriage, and I said we had always agreed we wouldn't.

Around that time I'd begun meeting this man for coffee or the occasional walk or glass of wine (we first met through a work project). I am going for transparency here, Sybil, so I admit it gave me a delicious feeling I knew I ought not to have, but I was angry with Felix and hurt, so I didn't heed the internal warning sense. I became closer with this man (Luc) behind Felix's back, only as friends, but it wasn't that simple for him, I realized later. He was falling in love with me. He told me, but it wasn't like that for me. In December Felix picked up my cell off the table because an alarm was going off for my medicine, and there was a text message from the man, and Felix went ballistic. I wasn't, I am not, in love with the other man, but Felix didn't believe that. He wouldn't let me say a word in my defense so he doesn't know that nothing came to pass between myself and Luc (once he kissed me, but I did put a stop to that), but again, I couldn't convince Felix. He's a skeptic, or superstitious or something. I love, and have always loved, your brother and when it all blew up with Felix seeing the message, all of that, whatever that was with Luc, was over. I flirted with fire and I got burned, but I'm not a fool. I was wrong, but I learned my lesson and I need you to help me find a way to reach Felix. Please, Sybil.

Stewart

Dezi Martinelli
138 South Carrington St.
Hasbrouck Heights, NJ 07604

October 4, 2018

Dear Dezi,

Learning about the circumstances of your father's death caused me tremendous grief, and my offering is small, but it's all I have: I am sorry.

I am enclosing one of the letters your father wrote to me from prison. I was moved by this letter, his articulation of how much he loved you and your brother. If you'd like the others, I'll send them as well.

Would you be willing to send me the address of your mother in Italy? I'd like to write to her, and soon.

Yours ever,

Sybil Van Antwerp

Sybil Van Antwerp
17 Farney Road
Arnold, MD 21012
USA

4 November 2018

Dear Sybil,

I am terrifically sorry for the long delay in writing. Thank you very much for sending the documents along regarding our father. Really, it means a great deal to me to have this information. You may think it mad, but I spent a bit of time looking for his brother, Eugene. He was quite a bit younger than Charlie. It appears he resides in a convalescent home in the north of California and he is ninety years old.

I will tell you a bit about myself, as you have taken the time to do for me, though it's really rather dull. I've never married and I haven't any children. I suppose I devoted my life to my work, my brothers, caring for Mum. I was in love once, but it didn't work out. At some point along the way, in my late thirties I guess it was, I had a moment of regret, but it passed. I've been content. I have deteriorating vision, a condition they say is rare and hereditary and it grieves me because it will put a quicker end to my work. Reading this over, it seems a bit sad that's all there is to it! A quiet life. There's more, of course, but I'm not exactly sure how, and the vision makes writing such a chore (and writing was always a chore for me). Would it not be much easier if we talked on the phone? Would you mind? I also had a thought, and perhaps you would think it mad as well, but I had the thought you could visit. Perhaps together the boys and I could impart some of the past to you. I cannot explain why Mum put you up for adoption, but I am sorry, in a way. Perhaps if we could talk to you about her, and give you bits and pieces of her story, it would help. It's not a good time just now, with the dark winter on its way, but why don't you come in summer?

Consider it. I'd be delighted to host you.

All the very best,

Your sister Hattie

Florencia Martinelli
84 Via del Porrione
Bergamo 03950
ITALY

November 10, 2018

Dear Ms. Martinelli,

Many years ago you came to my chambers at a courthouse in Maryland with your sons and begged for mercy for your husband, Enzo, and I extended none. I am an old woman now, and I have a few great regrets, and this is one of them. Someone I loved very much said once to me there is no parallel universe; there is no 'what could have been if only.' How I wish there was. I've now come to know the circumstances and manner of Enzo's death. I am sorry for the suffering my blind bitterness caused for you and your family. I wish there was something I could do, but I know very well there is no way to bring back the dead.

In regret I am yours ever,

Sybil Van Antwerp
former chief clerk to Judge
Guy Donnelly

Mr. Larry McMurtry
℅ Booked Up Bookstore
216 S. Center St.
Archer City, TX 76351

December 10, 2018

Dear Mr. McMurtry,

I hope this letter makes its way into your hands via your bookstore as I was unable to find your home address. I understand you live in Archer City. I have been to Texas once, Houston rather recently as a matter of fact, but at this point in my life I don't imagine I will go again. However, if I did I would want to visit your bookstore. I have admired you for years and imagined, if we had ever had the occasion to meet, say, at a dinner party, we would have fastened to each other like magnets.

It is my understanding that you underwent a heart surgery some years ago that had long-term adverse effects, and I am very sorry for the pain and trouble you have had in the aftermath. I have found it to be absolutely astounding, all the trouble living has turned out to be. Things nobody ever warned me about. I wish someone would have thought to say to me, earlier on, 'Sybil, over and over again serpents will emerge from the bottom of the sea and grab you by the feet.' Of course I didn't say anything of the sort to my own children, and I probably never would.

I want to tell you about my experience with having read Lonesome Dove. I have read the book now three times, and I'm sure you are aware of the short television series that was made, which I have also rented from the library a few times and enjoyed very much. Years ago I read the novel for the first time, as I said, when it won the Pulitzer Prize. I used to try to always read the prize winners, and indeed, I happened to read Lonesome Dove during a stretch of my life when I felt that everyone around me was rising up to the fullness of themselves while I was withering, and I will never forget the first time reading that book. It seemed to me that the text was tapping down into some ancient, painful stream of truth, or rather, the story of the cattle drive and its narrative appendages seemed to be somehow coming out of me, rather than going in. Do you think I sound insane, or (I rather think probably) do you know exactly what it is I'm saying? I remember reading that book and getting into, oh, I don't know, the last hundred pages perhaps, when you see as a reader that you are not in for a happy or neat ending for any one of the characters of which you have grown so fond; you're in for a hard ending, and you rather know that you are, I think. Or at least I did. And then it comes, you know, and I will never forget sitting there in my bed, with my husband sleeping beside me only a short while before he ended up leaving me, and I was sitting there thinking here in my hands is a book about disappointment. Disappointment for every one of these people. Wretched, bitter disappointment. And I was angry, of course, but it was really that I was dismayed by your mercilessness, the way you dished out blow after blow, refusing to yield, even a little, and provide the reading population with a sense of relief in any measure. It was agonizing because it felt so true to the experiences of my own life, and I suppose, back then, I was reading fiction in search of assurances that there was still reason for hope.

I think I probably wrote to you back then, or perhaps I meant to write but did not (because, as I said, this was a tumultuous time in my life and it's possible this one slipped by). I read Lonesome Dove again in the late nineties when another book in the series was published, and then over this past Christmas I found myself standing at the bookcase. I take great care with my selections now, knowing my years of reading are coming to an end. Seeing that familiar cracked spine, I was inclined to take the book down and read it again, and this is why I am writing you today.

I am an old woman and my life has been some strange balance of miraculous and mundane. This time, when I read your book again, prepared for the feelings I had felt before, I was surprised utterly. What I had seen those years ago as a lack of mercy became to me a presence of . . . courage—to hurt them! To leave them in dismay! It was courageous because it was unbearable but it was true, and YET, Mr. McMurtry. AND YET. Here was something I had not taken pains to see, but for which I was now looking, indeed hoping to find (as I am hoping to find in my own life): this GREAT VITALITY. Augustus and Call, full to overflowing with the meaning of the life they had made. The text meant something new to me this time around, and I wanted to say that to you. Yes, really, that's all. I wanted to make sure you knew that. I don't know what drives a person to be an author; I have no idea. But you should know that this text, this work of storytelling, touched something in me, lit a wick. I suppose I'm moved. That's what I am trying to say. You moved me.

And here, I know you are all tucked away down in Texas, and we are both caught in the wretched web of aging, aren't we, but I hope this last stretch of time we both have, I hope it is full for you. This is also, I suppose, what I hope for myself.

With very warm regards I write,

Sybil Van Antwerp

Sybil Van Antwerp
17 Farney Rd.
Arnold, MD 21012

December 24, 2018

Dear Ms. Van Antwerp,

Thank you for your note regarding Lonesome Dove. It seems that book has meant something to a good many people, and in ways I didn't even forsee, but I will say there was something in your letter I thought was interesting, that hurting my characters takes courage. That was interesting.

You're right what you said about the trouble it is to make it through life, but here we are, so I guess we've outsmarted something. I'm sure you're not as old as me, though. My bookstore is really more of a book town. If you do end up visiting, let me know, and I'll be sure to meet you in person.

All the best, and Merry Christmas,

Larry

Dear Theodore,

Thank you for trimming the high bushes for me yesterday. Your height is a tremendous asset.

As I mentioned to you a few weeks ago, I had broken things off with Mick. He was a bit much, and possessive, needing to be married. Imagine, needing to be married again at our ages. And he much older than myself. It is such a relief! I would have <u>hated</u> living in Texas.

In other news, I booked my flight to London. (First class! I have all this money—from people dying, no great accomplishment of my own.) I'll see Fiona for a week or so. She is going to take me up to see Oxford, and then onto the Yorkshire moors, which is where Emily Brontë set <u>Wuthering Heights</u>, and then she'll drive me north to Fort William to meet Hattie and the brothers. She's become very supportive of the madness. I'll leave at the end of April. If it goes well, if I find I enjoy moving about the world like a cavalier twentysomething, I wonder what would you think of taking a trip? With me, I mean, of course. I've always had a secret wish to see Paris.

In the meantime, more reasonable plans: it's been years since I went to the National Symphony, and I understand they are putting on Carmina Burana in late February. Would you take me?

Warm regards,

Sybil

January 27, 2019

My dear Sybil,

We didn't address this when we were together last night, but just
to say, I would be honored to accompany you to Paris.

Yours,

Theodore

Rosalie Van Antwerp
33 Orange Lane
Goshen, CT 06756

April 29, 2019

Dear Rosalie,

I'm off! Leaving tomorrow first thing. Bruce will drop me at the
airport in Washington. I have a few hours to wait there before the
flight leaves for London. I am a nervous wreck, but as I buzz
around the house there is nothing I've left undone. I washed the
windows and scalded the kitchen drain with vinegar and water.
Trash cans are empty. Sheets on all beds are clean and pressed.
My first time out of the country, and at seventy-nine years old! I'll
be sure to write—

Syb

Postscript: You should have a heavy box arriving at your doorstep in a few days. It's all the letters. Every last one, beginning
with the ones from when we were girls. I hope you will piece the
decades-long story back together. Who knows, maybe you could
sell the thing, although, as you said, I'm not sure anyone but us
would find it interesting. It should be quite a tome by this point.
Theodore had to lift the box to the counter at the post office.

Mr. Theodore N. Lübeck
11 Farney Road
Arnold, Maryland 21012
USA

May 11, 2019

Oh, Theodore. How can I describe it? I will do my very best, though the gluttonous eyes have nearly quit. They've seen a golden glimpse of heaven on earth, and now they demand rest (this is my first clear seeing day in a week, so I'm taking the opportunity to write). How to put words to my pleasure? What little my eyes have seen? I am home. The landscape soars, immense and distant and gentle, and the sky is crisp and alive, clear, moving, and textured, the air a raw quality I never knew existed. All the green, the stone, the water. My sister is wonderful, clever, and quiet. You know who she most reminds me of? Harry. Hattie and my three half brothers, well, it seems as if I've had all four of them all along.

I don't know how it is that I've waited until the age I am to begin traveling, and now being nearly blind, but then that's not true. Of course I know, and I want to tell you. I want to tell you something I have never told anyone. I should have. You'll see I should have once you've read what I have to say. Bear with me; my penmanship has gone to shit shit shit.

Gilbert did not die from drowning, as I told you, but now I want to tell you exactly what happened. I have never told this to anyone. I probably couldn't tell it, but I am going to try to write it. We took the children to a lake on the border of Canada for vacation. Bruce was ten, Gilbert eight, and Fiona four. We stayed in a lovely little lodge right on the water, two connected bedrooms, the children in the one room with two single beds, with Fiona always tucked in against Gilly, and Daan and me in the other room with a nice big four-poster bed and we had a view of the lake and a fireplace in the room. Rosalie and Lars came along, too, and Rosalie was hugely pregnant with Paul. We were served all the meals as part of the stay. It was July, so we'd escaped the wretched heat and gone on up to Canada by train. Can you remember how lovely it used to be, traveling by train? We were there by a small lake—Lake Saint-Pierre, in the French part, but Daan could translate for us. It was Fiona I'd always worried over (my baby, only girl), and the boys were always so capable it was like when I had Fi, in my mind the boys had grown up. And anyway, what happened is that Daan was playing chess with Bruce at the house and Fiona was napping. Lars and Rosalie had taken a canoe to a small island, so it was only Gilly and me down at the lakeside. I had been distracted all week. Daan and I had been arguing in the weeks leading up to the trip, an issue of our competing careers and whose would take precedence. I'd brought some legal documents along and that had bothered him because it was supposed to be family time and there I was with my briefcase, so I was sneaking work in whenever he wasn't around. I'd brought a file down with me to the little fishing dock there and Gilly had been sitting fishing for some time while I looked through the file, but he wanted to swim. He'd been patient. He was always very kind to me, Gilbert was. Quick to forgive, not demanding. That boy was so kind to me. Anyway—where was I, yes, he had waited patiently, but he started to beg and whine. He was a moving, athletic, energetic child, not suited for sitting still at all. I was absorbed utterly, making notes on the case, ignoring him. It was a case about a robbery, I recall. He asked me again and again, would I please swim with him, but I was irritated, being distracted, and indignant that I should have a moment for myself. I told him shortly that I would not, that I had to read the file, or whatever I said. I'm sure I raised my voice. It makes me sick to think about it now,

Theodore. Finally he asked me, if I wouldn't swim, then would I watch his dive and give him a score, and I waved him off, told him yes, to go ahead, I was working, but I would score his dive. There around the fishing dock the lake had been cleared of underwater stones and things, and it was deep, but they'd told us clearly that there were low, hidden stones and shelves all around the waterline, never to dive or jump from a place other than the fishing dock, and we'd told the children that, too, but Gilbert was fearless, reckless, and maybe he was punishing me for ignoring him, but I didn't see Gilbert step off the dock and onto the shore. I didn't see that he had climbed up onto a smooth boulder about fifteen feet away and that he was standing there so high. I heard him call out to me, thinking he was there at the end of the dock, or not really thinking of him at all, Theodore, I was irritated with him, and he said, WATCH. Watch me. Watch my dive, Mom. I wish I could remember, but here is where things go murky. I lose the trail in my memory, but one thing is clear, Theodore. Without looking up, I said, JUST GO, COLT. JUMP! It was the nickname I used for him. We were obsessed with the horse races, had loved to watch the horse races together. Secretariat had won the Triple Crown just the month earlier, and it was how I called Gilbert, my child, swift as a colt.

Sometimes I imagine it, his body folded against the summer sky, then stretching out, then down into the lake. Hands arms head body legs pointed feet toes toenails. I didn't see it, but I imagine it. There was a shelf there where he dove in. His neck broke and he didn't come up, Theodore. It took me a few seconds to register the lack of him. That's how Gilbert died, and I'm sorry. I am so very, very sorry. I'm going to put the pen down for a bit.

I never told Daan. I tried many times, I wanted to, but now he's dead. I'm sure it's why our marriage ended. I have wondered if

Rosalie knows. Maybe not the details, but my part in it. I've always felt she knows.

That was the end of many, many things, one of which was any desire I had to go anywhere. No more travel. Look at what Sybil on travel had turned out—a dead child. My second son, gone like that. You can imagine the aftermath: grief and guilt on repeat for forty years. I guess in one way I am a writer. I am a correspondent. It's been terribly difficult writing this, yes, because of my eyes, but also because it's a hideous story that would be better by far if it could simply be untrue, but here we are and I wanted to write it once before I can't write it anymore. I spent my life afraid, but now I am trying—trying not to be. After all, what is there to fear in the end, really? Loss? I've lost the most. Death? I'll welcome it. I am trying to drive the haunts out of myself and to the page. This is my last one.

I told my daughter recently that my grief has been an unbearable noise in my head for decades, and yet now, finally, I have written this letter to you and I'm surprised to find it is finally quiet.

There is a quote from one of my friend Joan Didion's essays. It's from the last essay in The White Album. The quote is: "What I have made for myself is personal, but is not exactly peace," and then it goes on, and then, "Most of us live less theatrically, but remain the survivors of a peculiar and inward time." This feels like the truest thing I have ever read.

I guess there's no bottom to a person, but I feel you have left fewer stones unturned than anyone else who's ever passed through, and it's taken me some time to recognize how knowing you has been like coming in from the cold, lonely road to find a warm fire and a table laid, so thank you for that, Theodore.

Hattie says I can stay here as long as I like. She lives in a lovely, flat house on a small loch, plenty of rooms. I wonder, is it mad for me to ask, would you like to come over to Scotland for a few weeks? You really can't imagine the cows here, like Chewbacca from the Star Wars films Harry had us watch. You have to see it to believe it. Furthermore, I wonder, when I get back, if you might want to just go ahead and move into the house with me. Why not? I need a companion, with my eyes. I know it's rather forward of me, but you said yourself that your house doesn't mean anything immense to you, and it's mine after all with the good view through the trees of the cove. Consider it. I'm being absolutely serious. Bruce even said we could spruce up your house and keep it for a rental property. Wouldn't that be smart of us? And with the money we make on the house we can travel—

It would be lovely if you were here. Of course you know I'm yours, have been for quite some time, with affection,

Sybil

TO: sybilvanantwerp@aol.com
FROM: jameswlandy@gmail.com
DATE: May 15, 2019 04:45 AM
SUBJECT: Harry, and other things

Dear Sybil,

I hope you are enjoying England with your daughter. I had you on my mind, and this morning, Saturday, and with little to do I find the time to sit down and fire off a message. I started reading. Well, listening to audiobooks mostly. I just finished *The Girl with the Dragon Tattoo* series of three books. Have you read them? They were great.

Harry will be in New York for the summer with an internship at a literary agency. I was hoping he'd come to Washington, but he's dead set. Marly's still in California, and I imagine she'll stay there. She's in and out of treatment, and her sister manages it while I pay the bills. The girls are off and doing their own things. I'm considering selling the house. It seems absurd to keep it. I don't entertain. You ought to come in for a dinner or something when you get back from your trip. It would be great to see you.

James

By the way, I was sorry to hear things fell through with Mick Watts. Had he proposed to you? I'd heard a rumor.

I'm going to be finished after this, darling. It's gotten to the point I don't enjoy the writing, gives me an awful headache and makes my hand cramp, I suppose because of the focus required now, and maybe it's silly of me to continue to address you, but it's—it hasn't felt silly.

When I started writing to you, it was in an effort to live—not just shrivel up and die—and it's worked. It's kept you beside me. I looked back. The first time was when Daan moved back to Belgium. Each time I've sat down to write you, I have imagined you sitting at some celestial desk and looking down over my shoulder, and perhaps that is absurdly delusional, but perhaps it is not. Perhaps it is not and perhaps it is.

You know, I imagine what it would be like if you were here. I've taken your personality, all that I knew of it before you were gone, and stretched it out as far as I am able. It's like trying to press out pastry dough as thin as possible without tearing it. I stretch you out to now, imagining you as a fifty-four-year-old man. However, what I have very rarely allowed myself to do is <u>remember</u> you. When I start to think back, I often slam the door—well. But this morning I was sitting in my sister's garden listening to the birds and the breeze and the cattle nearby, my eyes closed, and a memory came to me, a gift, and I didn't slam the door. I allowed myself to remember. An afternoon one autumn I took you all down to the park, down that hill through the neighborhood past the houses, and remember they got bigger as you descended, and it got pretty steep (walking back home was monstrous). You always took off running full speed down that hill. You with your long legs would fly. It was miraculous. By the time you were this age, six or seven, you know, it didn't even concern me anymore, you were like a limber bolt of lightning with that blind assurance and comfort in your body. Anyway, at the bottom of the hill that path along the stone wall, just lovely there, and then you would come out under the shade of that magnificent weeping willow tree. It was like heaven. I am thinking of this one afternoon when the four of us came into the park and you all went to do the things you often did—you and Bruce climbing one of the gnarled oaks, never pruned, massive limbs dipping nearly down to the earth, and Fiona searching for four-leaf clovers in the grass or sending leaves down the rush of the creek. There was one autumn when she was building a village from sticks and things for fairies, but I can't remember if this was that very same fall or not, but on the day I'm thinking of there was a homeless woman sleeping on one of the benches, wrapped up in various blankets and jackets, and her bag was beside her. She was facing outward and I can still see her face. She had an old dog that was awake and watching us. I'd never seen this woman before, and it was unusual to see the homeless around there. It was like she had wandered off her path and found herself somewhere lovely and just set herself down, but anyway, you and Bruce were startled when you noticed her. You know, it derailed you from your amusements for a few minutes, or maybe it was only a moment, and you did get back to playing, but I could see as I watched you play that you kept glancing at her, and the dog was following all three of you with its eyes. As we were leaving the park, the woman had woken and sat up and she was feeding the dog sections of a small orange. She gave us a nice wave as we left the park and she had these bright eyes. Isn't it amazing when it comes back, with the details? She was wearing an old red ski coat torn at the front with the stuffing, brown with filth, coming out. Later that night I was reading in my chair and you'd all been in bed for some time. I think Dad was already asleep, it was very dark, the fire had gone out, it was quite late, and you came to the study to find me. You were wearing long pajamas with red lines and you looked positively sick with anxiety. You couldn't sleep because you felt guilty, and I said for what, and you began to tell me. When we had come home from the park that evening and I'd gotten to work on the dinner you had gone to your room to count the money you'd saved in your money box in order to buy some toy or another (you were always saving up for something) and found you had forty-three dollars. I remember you saying that number all these years later. You told me you knew you ought to give the money to the homeless woman in the park, but you hadn't wanted to because of how much you wanted to keep it for whatever it was you were saving. And of course I told you it was all right, you didn't have to give your money away and all the rest, but you cut across me with the conviction you ought to have taken the money to her but hadn't, and you were ill about it. I tried to soothe you and in the end the only thing that settled you was that I said in the morning, if you really wanted, we could go back down to the park and if she was still there, you could give the woman some money. I figured in the morning it would have all blown over, but you came down the next day with a fistful of money and you said you were ready to go, so what could I do? I walked with you down the hill. The money bulged in your pocket. You didn't run, but you did stay about two or three paces ahead of me. When we got to the park, she wasn't there, of course. I admit I felt relieved. But you turned to me, positively in despair. We went home and got in the car. We drove around for a while, but there wasn't any sign of that woman and her dog. It was all forty-three dollars you wanted to give over to her, and you were grieved when you weren't able to. And you know, Colt, remembering that, I wept. For so, so many things, I could just weep. There is not language sufficient for me to express the depth of my sorrow for what happened, my son. Sorry doesn't begin to scratch the surface, but I think you know that. You would know that. Oh, Gilbert.

I considered going back to read all of it, this whole meandering opus, but it isn't necessary and it would be very difficult for me at this point. I think there are very many things I've forgotten by now, which is for the best.

When I started writing to you I don't know what I thought it was for. Maybe what I wanted was for you to know me. I have missed you all this time, of course, but the fact is that I got every moment of you there was. Enough of this now.

It is with love I've been writing,

Your mother

Sybil Van Antwerp
17 Farney Rd.
Arnold, MD 21012
USA

August 8, 2019

Dear Syb,

Please thank Theodore for transcribing your letters. I couldn't bear the thought of an end to our decades of letter writing, though now I admit I do feel a bit of a need to censor myself. He seems very polite. Stewart sends his regards as well.

Nothing much new to report, only had our annual Independence Day party here in France on the fourth, and it was a smash with women in the pool at the end of the night sans bathing costumes. We also got a dog—did I tell you that we were considering it? A little floofy white whatsit called Yvette and I love her. You would love her, too, though I know you don't care for animals whatsoever.

The big news is that the essay I'd been working on for quite some time on the expat experience we've had here has found a home in Vogue. I'm delighted. It is due to be in print come October.

Speaking of October, very much looking forward to your visit. Sybil Stone in France at last, I can die at peace. Have been mulling over the restaurants, etc. Just saw Eva at the party, and she was telling me they had new drapes put in. You won't believe her apartment, it will feel like yourself and Theodore hath died and opened thine eyes at the pearly gates. If I was visiting Paris, Eva's apartment is where I would want to stay, though she's never offered me two weeks there!

All my love, and kisses from the dog,

Felix

p.s. I must know. Do you share a room now, or does he sleep in guest quarters? (It's absolutely gauche of me to ask . . . and knowing it's Mr. Lübeck reading this to you . . .)

Postcard from Paris

Rosalie Van Antwerp
33 Orange Lane
Goshen, CT 06756
USA

Rosalie—Hello from the City of Lights! I know you loved Paris
when you were here in the seventies and I can understand why.
Theodore and I are having a lovely time. He has visited Paris a
number of times in the past and serves as a wonderful touring
companion. We are staying in a very well appointed apartment
belonging to a friend of Felix's with windows ten feet tall just
near the Tuileries gardens. Sainte-Chapelle was my favorite. I sat
in the pews and wept. Everything is resolved with Stewart and
Felix for the moment, thanks in part to Felix's successful essay in
<u>Vogue</u>. I tried the books on tape, but really cannot focus and de-
test the headphones and bad narrators, so not reading anything
anymore, though sometimes I have Theodore read to me aloud.
Miss you, sending love—Sybil

Hi, Rosalie. I'm taking good care of her. The vision problem makes her
afraid, which she won't say. She regrets she can't see details in the art, but
when the Eiffel Tower lights up, she can see that. Regards, T. Lübeck

Sybil Van Antwerp
17 Farney Rd.
Arnold, MD 21012

December 15, 2019

Dear Ms. Van Antwerp,

I am enclosing the first draft of my novel titled <u>Dynasty of Sight</u>. (Thanks for helping me with the title.) I probably would not have written a book if I hadn't lived with you that year. I know you can't read it, but maybe Theodore can read it to you.

I love you,

Harry

Rosalie Van Antwerp
33 Orange Lane
Goshen, CT 06756
USA

February 8, 2020

Dear Rosalie,

Thinking of you, as I always am. Spending the mornings walking with the dogs and afternoons in the garden listening to the wind and smelling the fresh highland air. My view of the river on Farney Road, which felt grand, was so slim. You have to see the loch to believe it. Fiona and Walt and the children, you know, were here two wonderful weeks over the holidays. Bruce and his lot are coming in April, then Stewart and Felix in June. Everyone wants a turn! I am happy. Hattie and I sit and tell stories in the evenings, and sometimes Douggie, Declan, and John come and we all sit talking about the past. We have so much to learn about one another. They love Theodore. Theodore read me the letter from January 20 and I'm grieved to hear of Lars's decline. It was the right thing putting him in Greenmont. You are right about what you said—we are thirty in our hearts, before all the disappointment, all the ways it turned out to be so much more painful than we thought it would be, but then again, it has also been magic. I miss you. Back in late April, and Theodore will accompany me for a visit. You're the only person left who writes, and I'm grateful.

Love,

Sybil in Scotland

Regards from Scotland,
Theodore

Hattie Gleason
Bodney Cottage
Fassfern
Fort William
PH33 7NP
Scotland
UNITED KINGDOM

November 10, 2021

Dearest Hattie,

It is with a heavy spirit I write in order to tell you that your sister, Sybil, passed away on Tuesday morning, what would have been her son Gilbert's fifty-seventh birthday. The doctors say she almost certainly died instantly when she suffered a pulmonary embolism. I am sorry to be the one to send this news, but the children asked me if I would.

You might wonder the details, as I would. She was fixing a cup of tea in the kitchen and I had walked down to the other house to tend the roses. When I returned after about thirty minutes, she was at her writing desk, the tea cold, her head lying on the desk as if she'd been ready to begin writing the way she used to.

Fiona and Bruce will go through Sybil's things in due course, and we will send along certain items you might like to have. The funeral services will take place two weeks from today at the church where Sybil was a member, Church of the Good Shepherd, Annapolis, in the event you would like to attempt attendance.

I am terribly sorry, Hattie, to deliver this devastating news as well as for my failure to be there at the final moment. I am grateful we were able to spend so much time with you in Scotland, and I am heartbroken that I didn't get more time with our Sybil (I am certain you will feel the same). It pains me to think of her alone, possibly afraid, and yet perhaps it is as she would have wanted. Her life, she said to me only very recently, had become so full these last few years, and yet I know that from certain things, now she is free.

I hope to see you again.
Your friend,

Theodore

p.s. I am enclosing a photograph of you all at the pub. Fiona took it the last time she was there.

Mr. Dezi Martinelli
138 South Carrington St.
Hasbrouck Heights, NJ 07604

November 25, 2021

Dear Mr. Martinelli,

My name is Fiona Van Antwerp-Beaumont, and Sybil Van Antwerp was my mother. I don't believe you would be aware, unless you happened to read her obituary in the newspaper, that she died a few weeks ago. It was sudden, and a shock to us.

In the last few years my mother made me aware of the manner in which she is connected to you, or, bound to you I would say (although I don't think she would have phrased it in such a way). I hope you know how much she regretted the decisions she made at a terrible time in her life that so reprehensibly affected you and your family.

We've seen to her will, and it appears that she left you a sum of money. There is a note there in reference to this gift. She wanted me specifically to write to you and tell you the money really came from my father, and you should use it to do whatever you can do to help your son. That's all she said, and you'll see the check enclosed is—well, I hope it's a welcome surprise.

Thank you for whatever kindness you showed my mother. She told me your forgiveness had relieved a heavy burden.

I wish you the best,

Fiona Van Antwerp-Beaumont

Fiona Van Antwerp-Beaumont
2 Hamilton Terrace
London SE 28 8JF
United Kingdom

January 15, 2022

Dear Fiona,

I hope you are well, and Walter, and the children. I am getting along fine, though missing your mother very much, a sentiment I know we share.

I picked up a copy of the book <u>Rebecca</u> on your mother's shelf and inside it I found tucked a few scraps of paper. It appears to be a draft or an attempt at a letter to your father from your mother. I am enclosing the letter. Perhaps it will mean something to you.

There was something Sybil was trying to find a way to tell you, and it's a shame she didn't bring it up in time. I think after reading this letter you will have questions. I might know the answers.

I very much look forward to your visit in March.

Until then,

Theodore

Dear Daan,

Do you remember me sitting long hours at the writing desk? Here I am still ~~as if nothing has changed~~. Everything has changed.

I have tried always to say exactly what I mean or to come as close to accuracy as the English language allows. Words have rarely failed me, and yet I find myself sitting down to write you and not ~~having the slightest idea what to say~~.

Here I've put the pen to the page, but

for weeks I have considered it.

~~It isn't that~~

I'm sorry you are dying, but we are all dying. I'm sorry you are dying with cancer—it makes it more insidious, somehow, even though it's all a wash in the end. But cancer rather makes dying a more ravaging sort of experience you have to endure—I'd much prefer to be surprised, ~~hit by a car~~ struck dead by lightning or decapitated (swift; lights off; horrific, but not agonizing) and yet most of us won't have the luxury.

There's something I need to ~~disclose admit to you~~ tell you

I have a confession (never saw the value in telling you)

(What good would it do for you to know?)

~~I was to blame~~ You said there was nothing to blame, but I was to blame

You have a right to know that

You were right to blame me because what happened is

What troubles me most about losing you is ~~losing~~ knowing you are the last person who ~~holds my~~ shares my memories of Gilbert knows who I was, what I was always trying to do

who I was doing my best to be. But I have to tell you something

There were times I hated you, but it was always I

I have hated myself, and that was what it was

You loved me

I~~ did my best~~ I tried so hard to be a good mother, good citizen, good in work, good wife, but missed the mark each time. You deserve to know that when we were at Lake Saint-Pierre

Not that we have spoken much, but it seems you're the only person on this earth who knows me and knowing you are there ~~is a comfort~~ has been a comfort a great comfort and I will miss that. The things only you knew—who else will keep my memories and my stones when you are gone? But there is something you don't know

The stone I didn't tell you, I must

There is a massive behemoth wrecking stone I TOLD HIM TO

I ~~did not grieve~~ was primarily concerned with self-flagellation, a guilt that plagues me now, even as I write

So you see, my grief was compounded by my culpability

By the time our marriage ~~was ending~~ ended I wasn't in love with you anymore, but I have always loved you.

Daan, I owe you a debt for drawing close to Fiona and Bruce when I was unable. You are very good to have done that ~~for them~~ for me

You are a good man, a good father

At the end of things, when you left for Belgium I didn't wonder—by that time I wasn't in love with you—but you left my parents gave me away you walked away from me and with

But if you had known, I've always wondered if it would have ~~saved us our marriage~~ our life SAVED our life

Of course I can't send the letter I want to send. What I want to say I cannot say. I know that, even if I wrote a letter a thousand miles long it would not be able express the universe of the human soul—my soul THE LETTERS pages and pages to what end? I cannot say. I am asking myself to what end. It doesn't amount to anything at all, they are nothing, only paper with my scrawling endless, but ~~it's the way I~~ that has been the manner by which I make meaning, I suppose ~~writing the letters is how~~ I but even still I even with all the writing I still don't

I had my DNA tested, you would be surprised to learn

I am sorry. I am so, so very sorry

I am going blind, and it terrifies me. If I cannot see, what do I have?

You're gone. I know I'll see you soon.

ACKNOWLEDGMENTS

When I was still in early draft stages of this book, the six-year-old son of some of our dear friends grew very sick over a few months, then died. Time stopped. The horrific, wrecking events of that fall and into December, when we woke up each morning with the one thing on our minds, changed me. I sat quietly with Sybil during that time as the saturation of grief worked its way into our lives, where it remains. Losing Wade bore significantly on this work of fiction and in a way, this book is also to you, Nicki and Kent, with love.

The road to publication for me was long and plagued by terrible weather for years, but I was not alone. Many people have been generous to me and helped me along the way, too many to name, however I would like to list a few.

I will be grateful forever to Amy Einhorn, who bought this book with real enthusiasm, right at the moment I was ready to give up writing and go to law school. This was a turning point in my life, and working with Amy and her wonderful colleagues Lori Kusatzky and Rachel Berkowitz, as well as benefiting from the smarts of the rest of the team at Crown, Tara Timinsky at Grandview, Lily Cooper—all of it has been the most fun I've ever had.

A few years earlier, my agent, Hilary McMahon, took me on when hundreds of others weren't interested, and she told me *You have what it takes*. She never faltered in believing that, even when I did, and her assurance restored a lot of confidence I had lost. Now we share a friendship, which is what I'd dreamed of.

In Trinity, Carlo Gébler took me under his wing and gave me the gift of his time. His ongoing mentorship is inexplicably valuable to me, and his help on this novel was clear-eyed and transformative. Eoin McNamee tended my work with meticulous care, as if it were his own, and from these, and my other professors in the creative writing master's program, Claire Keegan, Kevin Power, and Harry Clifton, as well as the friends and colleagues I made in many of my fellow students, I learned volumes about the craft as well as the art of fiction, and I am indebted. That was a wonderful time, a perfect year in Ireland that enriched and altered the course of my life in so many beautiful ways. I carry it with me and look back on it in wonder. My heart is always there, in Ireland.

Others I'd like to recognize and thank for their help with this novel specifically include Peggy Kent and Mike Robinson, who helped me with matters of legal accuracy, and early readers: Ashley Hill, Margaret Ann Speakman, David Speakman, Tory Dickerson, and Francesca Capossela. My gratitude going much further back to Gray Wilson, Kally Punger, Inman Majors, Teri Brennan, and the late Joan Frederick.

I'm tremendously thankful for the many friends who have walked beside me on the road, reading my work, bearing witness to many drafts and failures and disappointments for years on decades. Thank you especially to Kelly Whitener and Kaili Emmrich, my long-enduring cheerleaders, and Sorcha Hamilton, my trusted first reader, singular and treasured. To my family, who kept believing in a future we couldn't see. My parents, Claire Ficker and Tim Ficker, my granddaddy, Jack Vellines, and my in-laws, Joyce Evans, and Jon Evans, who died before publication. To my siblings, Hannah and Kyle, who are very dear to me.

I'm so grateful for and to my absolutely brilliant children,

Jack and Mae, for their patience and love as they show me the magic.

I do not see a way I could have gutted out the long, difficult years if I had not had my husband, Mark, by my side—my partner in the truest sense, hip to hip and shoulder to shoulder. How grateful I am to have found you. You keep the boat right. As it turns out, I got everything I wanted. Every moment of my life with you has been a kindness, and that is why this book is to you.

James 1:17

ABOUT THE AUTHOR

Virginia Evans is from the northeastern United States. She attended James Madison University for undergraduate studies (2008) and Trinity College in Dublin, Ireland, for her master's of philosophy in creative writing (2020). Now she lives in Winston-Salem, North Carolina, with her husband, Mark, their children Jack and Mae, and her red Labrador, Brigid.